FIDELITIES

West Virginia University Press, Morgantown 26506
© 2004 by West Virginia University Press

First edition published 2004 by West Virginia University Press
Printed in the United States of America

10 09 08 07 06 05 04   9 8 7 6 5 4 3 2 1

ISBN 0-937058-94-7 (alk. paper)

Library of Congress Cataloguing-in-Publication Data

Fidelities / Valerie Nieman
        xiv; 152p.   22cm.
1. Title.

IN PROCESS

Library of Congress Control Number: 2004111042

Cover photographs and design by Than Saffel
Printed in USA by Bookmasters

FIDELITIES

SHORT STORIES
BY

Valerie Nieman

Vandalia Press

Morgantown 2004

ACKNOWLEDGMENTS

"Act of Grace" appeared in the anthology "One Paycheck Away," Main Street Rag Press, 2003.

"Pas de Deux" won second prize in the 2003 O. Henry Festival fiction competition and was published in *2003 O. Henry Festival Stories*.

"Mayapple" appeared in the first edition of the online journal Ray's Road Review.

"Control" won the 2002 Elizabeth Simpson Smith Prize for the best short story by a writer in the Carolinas.

"Housecleaning" in the anthology "Racing Home" from The Paper Journey Press, Fall 2001

"Himself," News & Observer, 2000

"Knockdown" in Kestrel, 1999; excerpted from the novel "Survivors," published in February 2000 by Van Neste Books

"Crunch," Arts & Letters, 1999.

"Something Like Delilah," Wellspring, 1998; winner of the Elizabeth Simpson Smith Prize for the best short story by a writer in the Carolinas.

"Learning to Draw With Perspective," West Branch, 1997

"Delivering the Message," The Kenyon Review, 1996

"Where Happiness Is Expected," Antietam Review, 1995

"Trout," Calyx, 1989

"Edges," 1988 PEN Syndicated Fiction Series, also printed in the Charleston Gazette-Mail

For my Jack, who has opened up the world.

CONTENTS

~

WORTH

~

HE SAW THE YOUNG GUY coming slantwise down the bank, and knew that he'd sit down next to him.

Doyle Strawser didn't like people fishing close by. He didn't mind the men themselves, their talk, even kids with their jittering around. It was the nearness of their lines to his in the water.

The man paused, looked out over the lake.

He set his bucket down but kept the fishing rods in his hand. The lake, recently thawed, was gray as steel where paint had worn away from steady handling.

"Mind if I set up here?"

"Free country," Doyle answered, then opened his hand out toward the water.

He'd seen this guy in his orange hunting coat, fishing too close to the sucking current of the overflow. When he went up to the car, the guy had shifted position. Now he'd come the rest of the way around the lake. He must have seen the fish Doyle just caught, the sudden wet pop as it twisted to the surface.

"Any luck?" The young guy swung out a line baited with a mealworm and yellow marshmallow.

"Some."

The second rod had a limp nightcrawler on the hook. Doyle didn't say anything about his choices. The man cast it out farther, and the egg sinker took it down fast, about three feet to the left of Doyle's bait.

He fished trout pond style, a small orange-and-yellow bobber clipped loose on the line between the tip and the first guide to indicate strikes.

He fiddled with the bobbers until they hung pretty deep below the rods, swinging lightly in the breeze.

Doyle dabbled his fingers in the lake and wiped them dry on his twill pants. He took a can of Copenhagen out of his vest pocket and pinched up a wad of tobacco, watching the young guy work at propping up his poles. Instead of using forked sticks or spiral metal holders he tried to balance them with piles of rocks. Slapdash.

"Not too bad of a day," Doyle observed.

The rocks slithered and one of the rods clattered down. Bent over, his face turned away, the young guy said, "Beats sitting around the house."

He settled the rod back on its perch and sat down, bracing his heels against the rip-rap.

Out of work, Doyle thought. Not any welfare bum, not with hair trimmed neat at the back of his neck, his cheeks raw after a morning shave. Probably one of the guys laid off from Hedwick Mine, no hope for him when ones with 20 years or more were let go.

One of the red-and-white bobbers that marked his own lines dipped a bit. It might have been the wind, the way it seemed to slide lower, but Doyle looked at the dimple where his line went into the water and saw it move toward shore.

He lifted the rod carefully from its holder, brought in the slack by easy turns.

The line rested still in the water.

A sudden run toward deep water and the bobber slapped against the rod; Doyle jerked back and the rod bent at the stop of the fish.

Doyle worked the fish in, estimating by the manner of the strike and the resistance that it was a rainbow, decent size. He reached in and lipped the fish as it rolled in the shallows. The hook was buried deep in its gullet and he twisted it free with a sound of gristle breaking and whiff of garlic from the scented bait. He hefted it, a bit more than a pound and a half, gleaming with water and self-mucus, soft pink along the midline shading to steel blue and up into deep green at the top of the back.

He smacked the trout's head against a stone spattered black with dried blood. The jaws opened, shut, and he hit it again. The first was a flat cracking sound, the second a dull thud. The pearly gill covers flared, quivering, and the freckled tail curled and then stretched flat. Doyle slid the trout into the bread bag he carried, beside two smaller fish, their golden eyes filmed. The young guy watched so avidly that Doyle felt guilty.

Doyle unclipped the bobber, rebaited the hook with a ball of yellow Power Bait and a red garlic marshmallow. He offered the jars to the fellow, who said thanks, but didn't reel in to replace his baits.

Out on the lake the ganders spread their wings out and stretched their necks close to the gray water, moaning. The females flew up and settled. Too far south, too early, the light too low in the sky. The ganders swam toward them.

Doyle spit into a hole between the head-sized rocks that lined the steep bank, on the side away from the young guy.

Two men in an aluminum boat trolled around the island, the electric motor silent but the movement flighting up the restless geese and ducks. The men were bent over as if they had to row, humped against the chill on the water.

The young guy picked up one rod, alerted by a bobber that trembled and jumped then went still. A sudden, sharp strike and he hooked the fish, not much weight from the look. Still, he brought it in carefully, workmanlike. It was a brook trout, belly fins sharply marked in white and orange.

"Never many of those in the stock truck," Doyle said. The brookie was slender, something close to wild.

The young guy dipped his hand in the water and grasped the fish gently around the body. Doyle had seen farmers like that, tender with animals though they were headed for slaughter. He extracted the small gold hook, then slid the fish back into the lake. Doyle must have made a sound, not realizing, because the man turned toward him. Doyle tucked his face down into his beard and watched his lines.

Tossing the fish back like it had no worth! There he'd been thinking about giving him fish, putting himself out to help him. Thinking maybe he was hungry, or had kids.

Doyle felt restless all of a sudden. He pushed himself to his feet and went up the bank. The dry strings of crown vetch planted over the rip-rap caught at the lugs of his boots. He straddled across the guard rail, legs stiff from sitting, and went behind the car to piss.

He opened the passenger door and got out the thermos of coffee, light from his earlier visits. As he poured into the plastic cap, he watched the young guy lie back gingerly into the slope. Out of work and fishing instead of looking for a job, but then he likely had unemployment. Fishing filled the days better, he supposed, than sitting like some did outside the feed store, flexing hands stiff from lack of things to do, settling deeply into the benches. Better than sitting in an apartment, looking at the stories on television and wondering how long it would take someone to notice his absence.

Doyle saw the clouds layering, contemplated calling it a day. Then he went back down, his feet careful against the irregular teeth of the rocks, and settled into his place.

"Think you had a nibble."

He said "Huh" and looked at the still lines in the water, the current toward the outflow making a soft V from each line.

"They put a good many in here?"

Doyle nodded. "Half a truckload from Bowden on Tuesday."

A thick tongue of fish, a stream like molten steel, fish and water poured out. Something to see. He remembered once when the lake had been all but frozen, a January stocking, trout dumped down the icy boat ramp, sliding and twisting their way to a patch of open water.

"They used to stock careful, diff'rent places around." Doyle pointed. "The little bay, the other side of the island, back at the inlet. Now they just dump them." Hundreds of them, thousands, surely thousands. They weighed them at the hatchery by the pound, not the fish, so many pounds to this lake or that stream.

A red-winged blackbird lighted on a cattail stem, flaunted its epaulets and screamed, "Oh you cheat!"

"Mostly rainbows," Doyle said, catching back the end of a thought. "They used to stock brown trout. I remember catching one."

That was when he was a kid. His uncles fished, not his father, and he went with them to streams over east where there wasn't any coal, any mine water to ruin them. Later he didn't fish at all, working all the daylight through at his father's store.

"They raise some yet," the young guy said, "mostly fingerlings to stock up in the mountains."

"Don't get up there with these legs. I just fish the lake. Pretty nice rainbows they put in, and a few brookies." His mouth clamped shut on that word, thinking of the shame of a fish slipped back into the water.

"You here when they stocked Tuesday?" There was a faint tinge of disapproval in the man's voice.

"There's fish enough in the lake if you know to catch 'em. No sense following a truck anyway – they feed them trout full before they leave the hatchery."

Doyle looked over at the young guy, who stared past his lines to a lake that might be a hundred miles long, so distant was his focus.

"What's your name?"

"Gene."

"Doyle Strawser." He stuck out his hand and the young guy gave him his, cold and dry, a firm grip.

"Harold Strawser Feed and Seed."

"Yeah. That's me."

He'd been named Doyle after his mother's people, but his father was held in such esteem, a farmer of champion cattle and clean fields, that Doyle was known as Harold Strawser's boy. Not Harlan, the oldest, who farmed the valley spread their father had farmed. Not the younger kids who'd scattered to find new faces in larger towns. Doyle was the second son – the one behind the counter when he was hardly old enough to see over it, learning the trade of the feed and supply store that his father's prosperity built.

People called him Harold's boy right to his face.

He came to hate it over the years, the way his father did things, the way the store was arranged, and he not allowed to change a thing. Finally when the store was his alone, Doyle found that he'd adjusted. He didn't see the need to repaint the sign, to change things. When Harlan came in for calf starter he would bang his shin on the pallet of mineralized salt blocks, as he had for years, and just laugh.

Doyle used to believe that he was needed at the store every day. He had a suspicion that when he left the store just disappeared. Then with the troubles at home, he'd started going away fishing, days at a time, and found that things went right along. The workers always had a vague look of surprise when he came back, as though he had some purpose they'd forgotten.

The young guy stood, stretched his back. "Not having much luck here," he said.

Doyle glanced down at the jars of proper bait he'd offered, but didn't say anything.

"Think I'll move on." The fellow wound up his lines and lifted his bucket, rattled his way up the bank.

Doyle stretched his legs out, pleased at not having to keep himself to a narrow spot. It was a relief to have him gone, to be done with the effort of carrying a conversation like rocks from one place to another.

He stuck his hands in his pockets and waited for a bite. When he'd about given up, his eyes half-closed against the wind and his nose dripping, a bobber tap-tapped against the rod and he set the hook. A small fish, 10, 11 inches. But it made four in the bag, and with the temperature dropping and wind shifting it was a wonder to get that one.

Doyle levered himself up from the bank. He climbed to the road, leaning into the slope, balancing himself between his fishing bucket in his left hand, his rods in the other.

He set his rods against the green fender of his car, had to catch them as they skittered away, too cold-fingered to feel where they would hold when he set them up again. Finally he got them aright.

He was draining the stale ends of coffee from his cup when the young guy walked over.

"Thought you gave up, Gene."

He shrugged and looked down at the bread bag moving with the last reflexes of the fourth trout.

"Got your limit there?"

Doyle lifted the bag. Four trout, that best one close to 20 inches, showed like gunmetal through the red and yellow printing of the Kettering's wrapper.

"You have pretty good luck."

"Good enough for today."

"You didn't stash a couple more, under the rocks?" He looked at Doyle slantwise, his thin mouth turned up at the corners, his blue eyes sly.

Doyle laughed, knowing better. "There's guys do that, but not me. Not sticking my hands down in those rocks. There's rats live in the rocks."

The fellow shook his head slowly.

"You're sure this is it, just the four." And Doyle, who had been suspecting, was sure when the voice changed, so that when the man brought out his ID – Conservation Officer Gene Titchnell, West Virginia DNR – it came as no surprise.

"You seen me catch 'em," he protested, rattling the tackle and stringer in his bucket, sure the warden had seen no more than those four fish.

The conservation officer stood for a moment, Doyle looking right back at him. Then he moved around the car, reached up under the wheel-well into the frame, brought out a fish and slapped it down on the hood.

"Five."

The vibration was enough to send the rods sliding, and Doyle, startled, lunged for them. Dark snuff-spit burst from his open mouth and onto his beard. He wiped the back of his hand across his mouth, rolling the wet tobacco from his lips.

Titchnell walked back along the other side of the car. He leaned down, looked, reached back under the leaf springs.

"Six." A trout caught first thing that morning hit the metal with a hard swack, its nearly dry skin sticking immediately.

Doyle took off his auction barn hat, worn and creased with daily handling, and ran it around and around in his fingers and then put it back on.

The officer checked the other rear wheel – nothing – and then asked him to open the car. Doyle did and stood aside, stiff with knowing that the men all up and down the bank were watching.

Some seemed not to look, but their eyes were bright under the bills of their caps. Others, interested in the spectacle, came up to their cars to get coffee, or to sit inside with the heaters running and watch.

He knew these men who fished Michael Run Lake, pretty much as well as he did the lake itself, the high earthen wall that kept it in, the brushy shallows and the deep hole. "Harold's boy," he could all but hear them say, "Harold's boy got hisself pinched."

Doyle pushed his chilblained hands into the pockets of his red hunting vest – held together with a pin, the zipper broken since fall. In the one side he had a carton of mealworms that he hadn't even opened, planning to take them home and add to the rest.

"Eleven," the warden said, the five trout stuffed into another plastic sack under the passenger seat.

If he lost his license, Doyle thought, watching Titchnell pick over his car, there wouldn't be any need for the mealworms. He had saved them in a five-gallon bucket, fed them bran he ordered special, and waited for them to turn into the black bugs that would breed more mealworms. Hundreds, thousands, without any need of the bait shop.

Titchnell checked the empty glove compartment.

When he pulled down the visor, a small brookie hung for a moment, glued to the bare metal roof, then slid right down into that bean-counter's face.

Doyle kept from laughing. In the shuddering loose mirror on the open door, he saw himself, tobacco stain on the white that had become the better part of his beard.

"Twelve."

The warden poked around the car. Doyle watched a commotion out on the lake, as two ganders flushed a female from the water. They honked but she was gone, circling to land well away.

The ganders beat their wings until their bodies lifted from the water, but they did not fly. The female cruised closer and they cried out to her. Doyle couldn't help but think of his own wife and her loud pleasuring. He mistrusted that, how Emily took such pleasure from him even after the kids and all.

She had her ways, not what people might think. Set in them. Finally he couldn't take her controlling his life, 28 years of her guiding him this way and that like a horse trained to fancy gaits. Gentle as a rein on the neck but there, always there. Last fall, the night of the first real snow, he left. She had the house with three years' worth of wood racked up, and the new Jeep and all the things that were hers in the house, that she had settled in their places and he supposed were there yet, undisturbed by his going.

"Twelve," said Titchnell, deadpan, "is three times the limit."

Doyle studied the trout laid out on the weather-chalked hood of the car. He was shamed by the sight of the stiff fish, the white spots where their skin had dried, the gummy flatness of their eyes. When he had pulled them from the lake they were pretty as anything, rainbows shimmering on their flanks, dark freckles scattered over, the fine pointed teeth in the jaw and the rasp of the tongue. It was God's bounty, the perfection of plenty, and he was meant to have them. He had devoted himself to this, in the cold and the rain, bringing this beauty up to the light.

Close to the island, the ganders crooned and flattened themselves to the lake surface. The geese turned away. They didn't pay any more attention than they did to the fisherman who cast and cast, the blade of his spinner turning slowly as it arced down, until it splayed on the water and sank. He reeled and cast, reeled and cast.

Doyle knew them, Pete who liked the spinners, Shorty, Gandy, Jim who used gypsy oil on his bait. They all hid fish. Fish they'd earned, fish their taxes paid for, not somebody out of Pennsylvania or Maryland. Some got their limit and took it home, coming and going four, five times a day when the stocking was on – there every day, hauling in the white-fleshed trout, fat with the indigestible bait they swallowed, corn, Velveeta, salmon eggs dyed green and red.

"I videotaped you from the van," Titchnell said, pointing out the painted-over telephone company van that had been parked along the guardrail when he got there, like something a man might live in were he down on his luck. Doyle supposed he should be impressed by the efficiency of the operation, but he thought it shameless. Sneaking, spying. A woman's look-through-the-curtains way of doing things.

"What were you thinking, Doyle?"

He despised this familiarity, as though it was allowed after an hour's fishing beside each other. Doyle stared across the lake into the brush willows on the far bank. A plastic bag, caught in the branches, shuddered in the wind and fell limp.

The warden was like the men who came into the store, the ones who called him Harold's boy, Harold's boy, and thought nothing of it. Thought of it as praise.

"Your license?"

Doyle got out his wallet. As the warden wrote down the numbers, he spoke up. "The address ain't right. Pine Street. 318-A Pine Street."

Titchnell glanced up, then crossed out the Rural Route address and wrote in the new one. He turned the license over to check for stamps.

They were all there, trout stamp and conservation stamp and all.

There was a difference in refusing to obey the law and accepting what skill and the water gave – like in the Bible, a net so full that it couldn't be brought into the boat.

The conservation officer scratched away on his pad of citations.

The trout were his due, earned by his expertise and loyalty, his special ability demonstrated, the fish coming to him as his right. In the freezer of Doyle's apartment refrigerator, they were stacked in foil and plastic wrap like ears of corn.

"I could confiscate your tackle and car, but I won't," Titchnell said.

Doyle stared down at his boots, at the dry vine trailing from the laces. So that's what the warden thought, then, poor old man. Doyle blinked at the heat in his eyes and didn't dare to look at him.

Titchnell handed him the citation. Then he took a black garbage bag out of his coat pocket and bagged up all the trout, slipping them into its mouth like so many bits of litter. Doyle supposed that was what they were, now.

He got into the car and started it. The engine shuddered in its odd pattern.

He drove slowly along the gravel road that circled the lake. This hollow was once a bottomland farm, the fields stretching back from Michael Run, until the flood control people saw the great bowl the land made here and raised the dam to fill it up.

The car smelled like fish, like always, and Doyle felt as though he was just getting here. The sky was gray as morning and he was empty-handed.

DELIVERING THE MESSAGE

⁓

Hilda decided that, having kept it to herself this long, she would wait and tell him after he'd eaten. Otherwise he would halt (she knows him this well) with the spoon slowly drooping in his hand, watching her, eyes mild and brown. Watching her, and not offering a word to help her get out what she had to say.

He liked his soup boiling. The chicken noodle soup, made from accumulated necks and backs and fence-jump-overs, was thin yellow, like fat under the skin. Bubbles rose from the bottom of the pot, rose and broke. The surface shuddered like a cow's hide, shaking off flies.

She sliced bread and laid each piece down, soft inside its crust. She opened a pint of chunk pickles. Outside, red sunset faded on the side of the barn, and the dusk-to-dawn light flickered and flared.

She did not see Lyle coming from the corn-crib, but she did see his big shadow, leaping across the frost-bitten lawn, the outline blurred in the mingling of last light and jittery, blue vapor glow. Then she heard him stamping on the back stoop. The wall creaked deep inside as he leaned against it to take off his boots.

"Oh, that smells good," he said, coming in, the words a satisfied sigh.

Lyle went to the sink and washed. When he sat down at the table, his gray hair was wet and iron-dark in front, and his hands carried soap smell in front of him. His clothes breathed out coolness and the aroma of the barn – cattle, the summer's timothy hay, molasses-laced grain. As she set the soup bowl down, Hilda rested her hand on his shoulder. Scratches from the harvest of fall raspberries were fading from her knuckles, new scars over a lifetime of others.

She sat across the kitchen table, in her place.

"Bread?"

He nodded and took the plate. A bit of grease shimmered at the corner of his easy mouth.

"Been thinking about the steer for slaughter," he said. "I think I'll send Snowman over to Jim. He's got three, four nice steers the same weight, more or less. Don't matter which he'd want to trade back."

Hilda nodded to her plate. She could have had the Charolais steer slaughtered, and eaten him happily, steak by steak, but Lyle was tender about his animals.

"That okay with you?"

"He's mean," she said, less mindful of the conversation than the discovery that the cabbage-roses on her dishes almost matched the pattern of her dress.

"Exactly what I was thinking. Always crowded the others. Best to be rid of him, before he crowds one of us up against a wall some morning."

She took a couple of sups at her dinner, because he was watching her. When he finished she took up his bowl for another helping.

As she stood at the kettle, stirring the soup, bringing banners of noodle up from the bottom, she thought maybe she should tell him. Now while the words waited at the back of her throat like a cough. Hilda poured one ladleful, carefully into the bowl.

"Lyle," she said.

"Hmmm?"

She filled the dish, but set it on the counter and did not turn.

"I have ...." Fear clamped onto her tongue. She swallowed fear down, to start again.

The telephone rang. And rang.

Lyle looked at her, surely wondering when she was going to answer it, then pushed back from the table. "What's that again?" he asked as he went into the front room.

Her shoulders tightened.

He stood with his hand on the receiver for one more ring.

"H'lo. Well, Claude."

Claude Flesher. He was a slapdash farmer, as his father had been.

Never built new fence when he could cobble the broken places together with snares of barbed wire.

"What's the problem? Yeah?"

She looked out the window. Pitch dark. She could see the one pole light at the Flesher place, well down the road, and closer but half-hidden in pines, intermittent with the movement of heavy branches, the lights at their nephew Jim's. She wondered if he had been called already.

"She down?"

No, this would be the first call Claude made.

"OK. OK. Be right over."

He hung up. "I've got to go."

"To Fleshers?" She felt her face tighten. "What's wrong now?"

His brows came together as though her peevishness was an unexpected nutshell his teeth had found and crunched.

"He's got a cow down. First calf, and I'll lay odds he's bred her too big."

Hilda poured his soup back into the kettle, but didn't say anything.

He sat on the one step going down into the back entry, next to the washer and dryer, and pulled on his boots. He put on his barn coat, a stained old Carhartt with a corduroy collar and frayed cuffs. While he did that, Hilda got down a wide-bottomed travel mug, one of a pair that Beth gave them for Christmas last.

"No, no." Lyle waved off the coffee. "What was it you were saying?"

"Nothing."

"No, before."

She felt pride creep up her spine from a cold knot at the small of her back.

"Nothing. Now go on."

"Well – don't worry about the soup." He looked at his emptied bowl.

"I was going to make a pie, after," she admitted.

He beamed. "I'll just have a nice warm piece of pie, then, when I get back. Shouldn't be too late."

~

Apple slices dropped into the bowl, bottoming against the gleaming stainless and then tipping their way up through the cold water.

The television eyed her bleakly from across the room. She didn't need that noise, not like these young women. Sometimes of a morning or an evening, when she was alone and working around the house, she'd sing in her voice that caught and broke too much for public ears. Hymns, old tunes, jingles for burger places they didn't have in the closest town, Christmas carols. Sometimes a sketch of song wouldn't leave her mind for hours. This morning, when the sky was a wind-washed March blue, she'd heard the slow church melody, "Fair are the meadows, Fair are the woodlands, Robed in flowers of blooming spring ...."

The slices of Cortlands from their own orchard fell into the bowl. They were all the same thickness, to bake properly. I can make certain of some things, she thought.

Anger surged back, another hot wave like the ones that had rocked her body at the change of life.

Of all nights for him to be gone! All the nights he sat here and laughed softly at the wry faces on the television, while she snapped beans or mended, and they exchanged hardly a word or needed to.

Of all nights.

They'd never had any children. Somehow that made Lyle the one that people called for help. He could've used help a time or two, but would call none but Jimmy, and him seldom. He'd take the offered hand but not ask. People like the Fleshers never had any problem asking, though. And Lyle was good at nearly everything – carpentry, tree-grafting, mechanics, plumbing – but especially he could handle animals. It was a talent, handed down from his father like water-witchery in some families.

The paring knife went deep and chunked out a piece of the core. She fished it from the bowl, dripping, (the slight smell of lemon juice roused), and cut it clean, waste from good.

Now she'd never made herself available that way, always to be running, though it would have been easy with the church and all. Who was to do here? Who to take care of the house and drive the tractor besides?

A car came from down the road, and slowed by the driveway. Hilda tilted her head forward to see past the curtain. The car speeded up. Must have been looking at the mailbox, to find someone by name now that it was dark and the white-faced farms grazed in their fields, alike without the sun to find fault.

She'd gotten the call just after noon. It startled her. She looked at the clock and thought, how strange, lunchtime.

"The doctor would like to see you," the nurse said smoothly. "We have an opening Friday."

"But I was just there."

"The doctor would like to discuss the results of your Pap smear."

"Now what does that mean?"

The nurse (one of the Owens girls) made a soothing noise and offered an appointment time.

Hilda cut her off. "My sister died of cancer. I want to know if it's cancer."

"I'll let the doctor talk with you," the nurse said.

That was it, of course, just like Zella. Cancer.

But Hilda had gone on to the monthly meeting of the Miriam Circle, and gave the lesson she'd prepared. No one noticed anything wrong – she'd checked her hair in the mirror, that no curl was pressed or astray, and that her blue eyes were clear and direct as always. She did not want their solicitousness, and her name on the prayer chain. Not yet.

Of course, the circle wasn't what it was some years ago. A few younger women had joined, but not enough to fill the places of ones Hilda grew up with, now gone. Sold out, bankrupt, farm divided, widowed, moved to Florida, moved to some city where their children lived.

Miriam, Sarah, Martha, Priscilla. She thought, as she often did, how the women in the circles seldom matched those stalwart namesakes. Lorena Olafsson who had been a Martha for decades was no housewife, while Ellen McGrath, president of the Sarah group, had seven kids and was barely thirty.

She filled her lap with another half-dozen apples. The shoulders were blackened by some blight that Lyle could tell you the name of, but it didn't affect the sweet flesh inside. She peeled it off, skins red and green and sooty.

Sarah. She'd always been partial to her story, though this most recent young pastor (for all his liberal ideas) would likely be shocked to know why. Hilda held a picture in her mind of the great camel's-hair tent making a hot darkness, and Sarah inside, laughing at the news. Laughing in secret, away from the sight of her husband if not God, rocking and holding it in, like a child herself in helpless merriment. Tears streaming down her lined face. Likely even pissing herself. And at the door, pompous Abraham playing the man of God. Old fool! Who twice had said she was his sister, no more than that to him, and got into trouble for his lies.

Hilda had never understood that part. Why Abraham wouldn't claim Sarah as his wife, even when she was ninety and pregnant, surely no object of desire then.

Two became one flesh, as they said at the marriage ceremony, but no one said that it would be so hard, the pulling and the tension like scar tissue from an old, accepted wound. Knowing that not a breath you took but affected the other. She wondered if the way her breath caught in her chest, now, made Lyle faint as he labored in Fleshers' barn. Not likely. It wasn't the same for men.

Her change of life had come and gone pretty easily, taking with it the last hope for a late child. Why had this news, and what would surely follow, come as such a shock? If she should lose her uterus, now, what did it matter? It had no more significance to her than tonsils to a five-year-old.

Hilda considered the emptiness that would be there. Would she fall in on herself like a crushed can? A fallen cake, or a mouth without teeth? She'd been proud of her small waist as a girl, though now she was thick across the middle.

The old people said that a big wife and a big barn never did a man harm.

She took up the last apple and peeled it, carefully not making a single peel all the way around. She cut short arcs and let them fall into the pan. As a girl she'd made long magical peels, all the way around, and thrown them down to make the initials of her true love's name. Once she got the letters MW, but thought it insignificant. Who knew the Wilcox boy was really named Morcar Lyle Wilcox?

She remembered finding the letters for Howard Baxter, and Pete Zeigler, both of whom she'd thought pretty swell at the time. But she and Lyle had weathered well together, as browned and wrinkled as two apples from working side by side in the fields. Pete had died last year. Cancer.

The apples were done, and she sat for a moment, reluctant to face the cheerful cinnamon and the business of crust-making. She looked out the window but the road was dark. And she refused, absolutely refused, to listen to the mantle clock ticking. That would be too much like the smug little stories in the women's magazines she read at the doctor's office.

Lyle insisted that she get a checkup once a year. She hated Dr. Ganick's rubbery hands, which seemed to have been permanently gloved, and the harsh light that made the paper gown a fiction, shadowing the creases in her skin as deep as Claude Flesher's eroded creekbanks.

In the waiting room she had to divert herself, and it was the women's magazines or else Bible stories for young readers, and those she knew well enough. The pictures only showed children with pleated tunics and curls (clean, every one) and a shining Jesus in white garments swathed with a red cloth that seemed to have no purpose. But the sick and the lame crowding close, Hilda imagined that all too well, Jesus with drawn face and dusty feet, and no one to hear of His weariness and His forebodings. Jesus wanted only to lie down in the boat, off from shore, and let the storm bear Him and His sheep-like companions away.

Hilda shuddered, thinking on, thinking of the poor disciples, sea-drenched and afraid, and believing themselves alone as though the one they confessed had never come to them.

She knew how Zella felt, now, when she'd said that she felt less of a woman with her uterus gone. At the time, she'd patted her sister on the hand and told her it was just temporary.

Her womb had never yielded Lyle a son or daughter, but he'd not reproached her for this. She had blamed herself, and grieved. Maybe this was the answer to it all. Maybe some slick of illness had been there all along, invisible as ice. She wondered how long she'd been incubating this formless child. Surely Lyle would wonder the same thing, and she flushed with the shame of it.

I've been a good wife, she thought fiercely. A good helpmate, not sickly, not pining. I've done my share.

She pushed down the thought that followed: I deserve better. I deserve to have my husband beside me in my hour of trouble, and not be abandoned on this night. She glared at the telephone, black and hunch-backed on its spindled stand.

Hilda carried the heavy bowl of sliced apples out of the kitchen. The water that had kept the exposed flesh from browning slopped and sang on the metal rim, lapping over to wet her apron.

She took out another bowl, the red-handled rolling pin, pastry cutter, lard and flour. She worked the dough up quickly. She rolled it out with long firm strokes, out and to the side and diagonally, keeping it round.

Hilda folded the crust in half, and half again, and picked it up. It was a tender weight in her hands.

Just that suddenly, the idea came that maybe Lyle would want no more lovemaking, her being mutilated and all.

Hilda dropped the dough into the tin and held her floured hands together, clenching them until the shaking passed.

She let her breath out and the tears didn't follow, despite the sharpness of the pang.

We've lived well enough together without children, she told herself. I suppose we can live well enough without that.

~

The pie had cooled by the time he made it home.

She heard the gravel crunch in the drive, and the race of the pickup truck's engine before he shut it off. She slid a scrap of paper between the pages to hold her place and went to make coffee.

He took off his boots in the entry. Hilda, looking up from the set-ting-out of pie and plates and silver, saw that his coat was streaked with blood or afterbirth, all down the shoulder. There was a raw smell about him now.

"I'm going to shuck this stuff right here," he said.

Hilda nodded.

Lyle dropped his overalls, unbuttoned that thin blue flannel shirt which, she saw, finally had split at the elbow. She hoped it hadn't been like that when he went over.

She took the clothes (that thick briny odor, sea-changing the warm cattle smell) and put them straight into the washer. He looked oddly thin, standing there in his undershirt and shorts, pale except for hands, face and throat. The hair on his chest was nearly all gray now. When they had married, he had been bare-chested as a girl.

"I'll just get you some clothes." She fled to the darkness of their bedroom, rummaging in the closet for longer than required.

As he put on the clean shirt and pants, she saw a streak of blood along the line of his jaw. Darkening but still red, still obviously blood.

"How was it?"

"Like I said. He bred a little heifer to some big sort of bull, I'd dare say Simmental though he wouldn't." He soaped hands already washed at a cold barn-tap, reddened and scraped. "Shame on Claude for his greed that he'd do such."

"Maybe he didn't think," she said, wanting to put an end to his talking, push away the puzzled ache in his voice.

"A fine calf it would've been." He shook his head. "The cow will make it, so there's not that anyway."

"You've got some dirt on your jaw."

"Where?"

"This side." She pointed to the place but didn't touch it.

He scrubbed his face hard, right up into the hair, around the neck, wetting the fresh shirt. Hilda got out the can of Bag Balm and set it on the sink, to ease his cuts. They must have used a calf puller; she thought she could see the imprint of a chain in the bruise across the back of his hand.

He splashed the last of the soap from his face, shut off the water and turned toward her, not twisting around but setting one foot square and then the other. A long piece of hair had fallen over his brow. He held his hands up, dripping, like a surgeon to be gloved or the pastor readying communion, or a man waiting for the child to come into his hands. Hilda brought the towel. He squinted as he opened his eyes against the soap-sting.

"Thanks, Blondie-Gundie," he teased, a decades-old nickname using the forsaken end of her given name. He dried his face and peered at her over the top of the towel.

He smiled then, his face clean as a boy's before church, shining with pain and trust, and his brown eyes full of all the willingness in the world.

Hilda went back to fixing pie and coffee. The knot of control in the pit of her stomach, where she'd held herself against crying all the afternoon and evening, relaxed.

He's been like Abraham, she thought, always ready for the miracle.

But what the Bible didn't say was that Abraham had loved Sarah. Plain as that. He'd been happy with her as she was, despite her hot, demanding anger, and she with him despite his lapses into fear – the heavenly message didn't do one thing to change that.

"Come sit, Lyle." She pulled out his chair. "There's something I have to tell you."

SOMETHING LIKE DELILAH

~

SUCH A THING CAN'T BE REFUSED, but Leora would have refused it just the same.

The mink coat came out of the box as though alive, the fur expanding, each hair standing alone and gleaming in the hazy sunlight. She caught up the rolled hem just before it lapped into a wet dab of dinner on the oilcloth.

Plastic tablecloth, she corrected herself. There hasn't been oilcloth for years and years.

She breathed in the strange scent of dead fur, of a vault full of beautiful skins. They tried to take the animal out of it with some kind of scent, but it remained stubbornly animal. Otherwise why would rich people want to wear a fur?

"A bequest," the letter said, "from the former Evelyn McIe to her classmate Leora Hibbs Withrow."

Leora pushed the coat back into its box, printed in black with the name of a furrier in Buffalo, N.Y. The fur rippled and bulged over the sides, slick as a cat's back and as insistent. Finally she got it all into place and pushed the box across the table.

She moved around the kitchen. She put the dry dishes away. She refilled the flour canister and wiped down the counter.

The bread she had baked in the morning was firm and cool. She wrapped three loaves and took them out to the side porch and the big chest freezer. The cold billowed when she lifted the lid. Another layer of frost settled out of the humid air and coated new containers of peas and chard, last fall's white-papered packages of beef.

Closing the lid, she looked out the window toward the barn, and there stood Vaughn. He held a broken branch in his left hand and was idly whacking away at the weeds. Pigweed and purslane fell over, broken, and green streaks showed on the faded white of the barn. His big head was down, studying, so that he looked for all the world like a boy at his doings. Then he threw the stick aside, picked up his purpose and walked toward the machine shed.

Leora shook her head. No accounting for them, she thought. She pushed once more, hard, on the freezer latch.

She took a case of jars from the shelf over the freezer, chasing off one of the fragile spiders that lived everywhere in the side porch. Might as well get the quart jars washed and ready for the blackberries.

But coming through the door she saw the coat again, its soft shoulders like sin itself, and Leora swelled with a mixture of excitement and grief.

She set the jars aside.

Such a gift. She bent down and rubbed her cheek against the fur. She felt warm, low in her body, as though she were the one being touched.

Leora carried the box to the bedroom. She lifted the mink coat out of the box, such a tender weight, and laid it across the bed. The sleeves were cuffed, a thick band of fur. The lining was a soft color somewhere between lilac and beige.

When she put it on, the mink settled around her so easily. Leora pulled the deep collar up and it framed her face like a movie star's, how they always looked to be made out of light even in flat magazine photographs. Skin like a pearl, the incandescent tip of each mink hair.

She turned this way and that. The mirror on the old bureau was white at the edges. She walked into the room and her image moved in the glass, shuddering with the weight of her footsteps on the loose old boards.

What would Vaughn think?

He knew about the coat, of course, had seen the letter and then the package, but knowing about something and touching it, breathing its scent, that was something different.

What would Vaughn think of her, in this coat?

She tilted the mirror on its dowels, so that she could see the whole body of the coat, though not her face any longer. Her fingertips, blunt like the claws of an old bear, showed at the edge of the too-long sleeves.

The shading was so careful, the joining of the skins so skillful, that the coat moved as though made out of a single animal. It flowed. The letter had called this a "fully-let-out Natural Autumn Haze mink." The appraisal figure that followed took her breath.

Leora stroked the flank of the coat, feeling her own shape made rounder, desirable, through it.

She thanked Evelyn in her heart, the Evelyn she remembered, huge green eyes and a brown charity dress. "But you might have sent something more useful," she added, knowing there were certain dangers to accepting gifts.

She couldn't wear it to the store, or the Farm Bureau meetings. She couldn't wear a mink coat to church, all puffed up before God. Where did Evelyn think she'd wear such a thing as this? The coat could be sold, she supposed, maybe in Pittsburgh, but it was a dying woman's wish, and sacred.

For a moment she wondered if the fur wasn't a comment on how far her friend had gone, reminding Leora of her own stay-at-home life with the less prosperous of the Withrow boys, but she wouldn't have believed that of Evelyn in life and certainly not after death.

Leora saw her bare briar-scratched ankles below the rich woman's coat. She was thin again as she'd been as a girl, but her hair was gray that would go to that same yellow as her mother's instead of white.

"Just Leora, and that's all there is to it."

She turned and looked at the coat, not seeing herself any more, seeing Evelyn – a tall, skinny girl who became a tall, elegant woman. Who went away and married well.

When they were neighbors on Vinegar Hill, the boys at school used to taunt her, "Ev-vie, Ev-vie, wants a Chev-vy. Ev-vie, Ev-vie, wants a Chev-vy." Only two families on the hill had cars, and they were both Fords, black and plain, yet enough to envy. But Evelyn wanted the pretty things from the start. Leora imagined her riding in a Cadillac, a white Cadillac with white leather seats, so much beyond the blue Chevrolet in the showroom window where Evelyn had paused every day as she walked from school to her job at Kroll's Diner.

Leora sat down on the bed, and the fur moved around her. The weight of it. She wondered how many minks were in it, being such narrow creatures.

The lining, at first cool and slippery, now was sticking to her neck and arms. It was just a mortal swelter to put this thing on at all in the summer. Leora folded the coat back and tucked the tissue paper around it. Then she lifted the box back to the top shelf of the closet, almost losing her balance as the weight of it tipped back, but with a bit of a push it fell flat.

∼

Pickling salt.

Leora passed the aisle with the pet supplies, the one with the general kitchen implements. They still carried those big yellow bread bowls, heavy pottery decorated with bands around the rim, like the one from her mother she broke 20 years ago and cried over.

The next aisle held the canning supplies – shelves stacked with pressure canners, lids, spices, enamel kettles, Ball Blue Books, cheesecloth, jars of Certo. Musgrove Seed and Feed had expanded over the years, without building on. Everything was jammed into the space available or hung from the bare old rafters of the high ceiling.

Through the noise of a mill grinding in the background and kids shrieking over a display of BB guns, she heard men's voices approach up the other aisle, a low rumbling like a creek after a heavy rain.

Fred Musgrove pleaded his case on higher prices for something or other.

"I'll just have to do 'thout, then."

That's John Lewis, she thought, picturing his cowlicked gray hair and wind-reddened cheeks, like a boy made up as an adult for a school play.

"It's like anything else, you think you gotta have it but come to find out, can get along anyways," he added.

"Well, I'll just say that some things you can do without, and some you're gonna have to pay for, like it or not," said Musgrove.

Leora smiled. He didn't like to lose a sale, took it personal if a customer refused an item. His ears would be red and he'd be chewing on the ragged inside of his lip.

"Maybe so." John Lewis paused. "Go ahead with the fence charger, though. Monday, if you could. Got the boy home to help set the new line, and then some ear-tagging to do."

She should pick up her salt and get along, Leora told herself, but it was sweetly forbidden to listen and she was enjoying it.

"Your herd looks good, John Lewis, when I been by."

"Calving went off well. My Ruby, one that took Reserve last fair, dropped twin calves just pretty as you please. All told, it's been a good enough year."

She continued to stare at the lids and rings, jar lifters, strainers. Pickling salt. The familiar girl under her umbrella. Leora squatted down, her knees cracking, and picked up one of the five-pound bags, checked to make sure it didn't leak.

"You heard about Pete Priester," Fred said, without any question in the saying.

"Can't say as I have."

"He left Susan, night before last. Just up and left, put his clothes in the pickup truck and his dog and was gone."

"No."

"Yeah, he did. I hear he's over in Hazelton with some woman, and not a soul suspected."

She was so close to the shelf that she could smell bay leaf and clove in the bagged pickling spices, the dusty cardboard smell of the red-and-white paper boxes of alum.

"Sue must have known something," John Lewis said.

"Not from what the women are saying. All the time he'd been driving over there of an evening to teach welding at the Vo-Tech, and apparently this was going on, too."

"What about the farm?"

"Her sister's boys are going to run it. That's what Maddy tells me, from church."

"I'll be damned."

Leora started to stand up, feeling the silence around as though the men had gone.

"If Vaughn wasn't there – if he was ever simple enough to leave like that – now I'd take up with Leora," said John Lewis, his voice suddenly strong and near. "I'll tell you that straight out."

She felt her ankles quiver with the length of time she'd crouched there. She ran her hand across the bag of salt. A film of dust cleared away, the width of her palm.

Leora waited for Fred to say something. She imagined his fleshy mouth, round as a doll's, purse and relax like it did when he was pondering.

She heard John Lewis start to talk again, the words fading as he walked away. His voice made her face burn.

She'd never imagined such a thing. All the afternoons at haying when she'd hauled out dripping jars of water for him and the other men to drink down at breathless length. At noon, she always cooked big meals, and he'd no more than nodded as he sat down to eat. That was sufficient, the men talking amongst themselves without much notice that their plates stayed full.

Just the other morning, his young stock had broken the line fence and she'd helped him round them up and drive them back across the fields. A heavy dew, and all the spider webs hanging as though to burst. They were drenched to the hips by the time the heifers were back in the pasture.

He'd had a word or two to say, the sidelong comments that passed in place of thanks between neighbors. And she was sure he'd been no different, he'd been just the same John Lewis Haden she and everyone knew, his voice the level same as always.

～

Leora turned off the gas and put the lid on the pot. Twenty-five minutes and the eggs would be ready to peel. The men would eat their pancakes, drink another cup of coffee and she'd have their lunches ready to take into the woods. Egg salad sandwiches. Slices of summer sausage. Apple pie, the Winesaps and Pippins yielding heavy this fall.

"A good frost this morning," Vaughn said, breaking out of his usual quiet.

"That takes care of the snakes, and that's fine by me. I never'll cut wood in the hot like some," John Lewis said.

"Makes me think of the snow to come, though."

Leora watched out the window. Maple's flame was giving way to maroons and purples, the oaks putting on the last color. The long shadows of the trees were white, holding onto the frost that the sun had burned away in the open.

"Maybe she'll get that fur coat out now," Vaughn went on.

She turned to the table as he said that, and as her eyes met his and Vaughn laughed, she flushed. It was not his familiar teasing glance that flustered her, but the way John Lewis looked. As though appraising her and the coat, considering the two together. She used to believe that everything a person thought was visible in his eyes, but John Lewis didn't give anything away. His eyes were gold, almost, a kind of hazel brown, and impenetrably clear.

Leora took the pepper from the table, lifted her head high and turned back to the counter.

She cut onion and celery, added dollops of mayonnaise. She felt the muscles slide in the backs of her legs as she stretched for the seasoned salt at the top of the cupboard. The house dress she wore was old and washed thin, and she knew it lay against her the way new pressed cotton wouldn't.

The men, absorbed in their food and consideration of the work ahead, didn't take any notice. They didn't see how squarely she cut slices from the loaf or hear the crack of the eggshells, the water tumbling over her hands. She cut the apple pie and wrapped wedges in foil. She felt like silence was all around her, that it shone out.

"You got chains enough?"

John Lewis said, "Two I just got sharpened at Musgrove's. I'm babying that saw along, though."

"Thought you just put a new clutch in it."

"I did, and it's not right, or that wasn't all there was wrong."

Leora made up the sandwiches, the egg salad still warm as she spread it, the bread crumbling at the edges.

She ran hot water in the thermos, poured it out, then spooned in the instant coffee. The kettle was boiling so hard on the high flame that steam pip-pipped through the whistler as she carried it from the stove.

John Lewis swigged down the last of his coffee and set the cup on the drain board.

"Thank you, Leora," he said.

She nodded. Vaughn took his lunch, gave her a squeeze on the elbow.

Leora waved as they left, pickup and tractor and wagon making dark tracks through the white frost and wet grass.

She went to put on her barn coat, to go out to the chicken house. The color of the corduroy collar, the same faded brown as ever, caused her to stop this morning. She hung the coat back on its hook.

Leora went to the bedroom closet and got down the box that had been on the top shelf for months. She lifted off the lid, unfolded the paper, let the mink rush out of its confinement just like before.

She put it on and the coat settled close around her shoulders.

She walked the circuit of her yard, the mink's heavy hem brushing with each step against the backs of her legs, a soft, repeated gesture.

Leora touched the quince bushes, unevenly round like their fruit she had picked and preserved. The mums were going brown, and the grape leaves were fox-colored around unharvested small bunches shriveled on the stems. In the garden, stumps of cabbage showed black, and the rags of the tomato plants. Weeds stood along the fence, wound into the sheep wire and unable to fall. The asparagus ferns were pale and dotted with red berries. Everything was harvested except the parsnips, last of all, waiting to be frozen in the clay and sweetened by the cold.

Chain saws stuttered up and the first one groaned as it bit into a tree.

Leora pulled the coat across her body, the house dress snugging cold against her cold skin. She knew how John Lewis would stand, his setter-red boots braced deep in the fallen leaves, his hands trembling with the work of the saw.

HIMSELF

~

HIMSELF, HE COULDN'T SEE THE SMOKE, that time of sky being blue and uncertain at the edges, but someone coming up the road surely would as they rounded the curve, see the curl of it against the dark lawn or the grove of pines grown tall, all of a height.

He smelled it, though. He knew the way it burned, slow to start, forever to go out, the fire laboring like a mattocks-man into the hard old heartwood of the locust stump.

The stump had been solid these years, on the lawn close by the road, sometimes making a newcome driver jerk the wheel hard, thinking someone stood there ready to leap the ditch and into his path.

The stump was weathered, but no weather would take it away. Not in his lifetime.

He'd put a match to it, he'd poured lamp oil to its center, he was taking the stump down level with the ground.

~

Years ago he'd cut down the tree that had stood on that stump, only because of his wife.

She was a large and solid woman. She sat in a chair with her hands on the arms like two roots on a rock. Deep in the chair, deep within the house.

She'd watched from the window, the trees, their growing. The shadbush and locust were young when they came there, new married, the trees already rooted close together as the wind or birds had thrown their seeds on the raw clay. The shadbush always frail in the bent black shadow of the other.

It took years for the growing, and years of her saying: I'd want that big tree down, now. It crowds the other and gives it no light.

He heard her and went about his business. All day while he was in the mill, she could have set an ax to the trunk herself. Gone from light to light, and when he came home, his shoulders twisted from the bend and pull of his work, she would sit across the table from him and say: That black locust tree, it needs cut. It's good only for fenceposts.

Finally he did it. The inside of the locust tree was yellow-green and smelled sharp as sweat long after the work's done.

∾

The stump, though, he left high, to be looking at it nights while he sat on the porch and the mosquitoes whined around his ears and the moths whirled, drawn by the blue light flickering from the television inside.

He liked how it marked where a tree had run deep into the ground, reminding him of himself. Not like his wife, spread wide as a cabbage across the earth, but running deep, himself all intermingled in the soil, roots threading down in the dark.

He could think how the rootlings forked into black loam until they came to an end at dog-yellow clay and bedrock, like the lightning forking white down out of the sky.

Once he heard how a lightning bolt, wherever it hit the earth, would boil the minerals and made a likeness of itself. The mark such as a hand might make, fingers spread into the mud. Every time lightning struck it left its trail behind in the ground, and he thought on that – all under the wide mindless surface, the electric fingerings, the path of it made plain and hidden at the same time.

∾

One spring night he looked out toward the road and the shape of the old stump caught at him. It hunched under the shadbush, which in its bloom spread white like someone wading to a preacher's arms to be laid back and baptized.

The shape of it. He'd thought, himself, the stump always stood as a landmark for their place. Now he saw that, worn down by the winters, it was round-shouldered as a man sitting with his hands loose between his knees.

~

Himself as he waited that night on a stump by the side of the road, on the raw acres where the paper mill had cut the pulp trees down like a stand of wheat and taken them away. The baked bare clay white under the moon, rutted with tracks, hatched with broken sticks and new-planted pines.

He had sat close by the edge where the trees weren't yet mowed down, and those were thick and crowded, black in their shadows, himself right up among the edge of them, among the resin smell and the gossip of them over his head.

And the girl came walking home over the back way. He saw her shadow first, jumping ahead of her in the moonlight.

She worked at the joint by the highway, wore the same white dress every day. He'd had eggs from her hand there, and watched her spread a sour cloth across the counter to wipe away the rings of his coffee. And he had conversation with her, caught that wide backward glance. The white of her eyes showed like that of a horse, excited.

So when she came by, her hair loosed down and her hand around the neck of a bag holding some leftover thing, he rose up and caught hold of her shoulder.

She could have run, she was a big strapping girl. But already she was set on the earth and so when he caught her, she stayed put, and so did he.

~

The stump sat by the side of the road.
And he had daughters.
Or maybe, the story goes, he had sons.

KNOCKDOWN
(EXCERPTED FROM *Survivors*, A NOVEL)

~

BUD CAME OUT OF FLUORESCENT DARKNESS into rain. The fall night was closer, darker; lights along the campus walkways appeared shrunken. The temperature must have dropped 20 degrees.

He tucked his box of punch cards under his arm, lowered his head so the rain wouldn't pelt his face, and stepped away from the building.

He was momentarily disoriented. He thought he might somehow have come out the wrong door, but there was the familiar flat-topped hedge of clipped hemlocks around the parking lot, and there was the hood of the Buick, slick and greenish under the lights.

Then he realized it was because he could not hear his own footsteps, lost in the rain.

It was almost like losing your way, for a minute, after hearing your own footsteps echo in the low buildings of the community college, in the slump hours between afternoon and night when the janitor pushed his mop bucket along on squeaky wheels and the only students were the bottle-plant men and a citizenship class with three old Italian women and an Oriental. Footsteps in those blank corridors sounded the same as they did when you walked by yourself at night along a deserted city street, too loud, too fast. Forty men coming out of a classroom at the same time, their footsteps didn't blend but stayed individual.

Bud pushed through a gap in the hedge worn by daytime students. Branches stroked his arms, leaving wet stains. He opened the car door and put the box of cards on the seat, shoved it over, and got in.

They were all glad to get out of there tonight, not because their stomachs growled with hasty dinners or the lack of them. It was the learning itself, now, too late in life for new ways of thinking, for paying attention to the placement of commas and periods. FORTRAN. COBOL. BASIC. Foreign languages, like seeing something written in Spanish with question marks inverted at the front of the sentence, or the long strings of Chinese down the side of fireworks.

Cars were coming into the lot, steady, like some kind of valve had opened to refill the emptying lot. He waited until one had manuevered into the space beside his, and then he shifted into drive and pulled out, easing past Win's station wagon. He saw tools piled in the back and wondered if he was working, getting a little cash under the table.

As he swung toward the exit, the punch cards slid across the seat and Bud had to make a grab for them. He caught the corner of the box just as it tipped toward the floor and at the same time tried to steer the car. He pulled the cards back, but the front wheel leaped onto the curb and rolled along it until the curb stopped and the car came down hard, scraping on the concrete.

"Judas Priest!"

He stopped the car in front of the canopy at the building entrance, got out and looked. There was a raw scrape on the paint, but no dent. Small favors.

When he stood straight, the long corridor extended in front of him, from the glass doors to where the wide panels had been pushed back at the entrance to the auditorium. The whole extent was full of light, like a fluorescent tube, and his eyes closed involuntarily against the glare.

He remembered, now, seeing posters for a lecture tonight. An intense, dark-eyed woman with hair cut close to her head.

Bud looked away from the corridor. The dome light in the Buick was faint; beyond the car, everything seemed uniformly black. He started to go around the front of the car and almost collided with a woman sheltering behind a plastic umbrella.

"Sorry, Miss," he said.

She lifted the umbrella above her head and seemed to hold her breath, drawing herself up to a little added height. Her eyes were bitterly cold behind the oversized round lenses of her glasses.

Bud ducked his head again and slipped into the car.

What the hell was wrong with her, he wondered.

He swung back around the one-way circle, checking to see if the car steered okay, into the parking lot and out again. He had to wait for a long string of traffic at Florney Drive. The pavement looked glassy under the headlights. There were leaves pasted to the dark surface.

When Cory had been in fourth grade – maybe fifth – he had to make a leaf book.

"I need at least twenty-five species," he'd explained. SPES-sies, he said. Bud had to sneak a look at his school book to figure out what he meant. They went to Great Bend Park, dark with pine and hemlock, and they walked into the second-growth woods at the top of Presidents Hill, heads down, looking at the leaves that had fallen. Cory kept sorting through his collection like he was playing pinochle, gathering all the maple leaves together and all the oaks, and then discarding this one, that one, for leaves with brighter colors. He liked oddities. A maple leaf covered with hundreds of little red tits, like seed warts. Oak galls. The star shapes of sweet gum, each one brilliant, maroon and yellow.

They found thirty-two species, and Joan ironed them between layers of waxed paper, with labels written in Cory's rambling longhand. The house had smelled like paraffin.

Someone honked. Bud jumped. A gap in the traffic closed before his eyes. The next opening was smaller, but he goosed the car and it skidded on the wet leaves, then swung into the line of cars headed across town.

He hit the lights in sequence, letting up on the accelerator just a little so that each one of them changed to green as he approached. He could see the lights go yellow on the cross street, then red. The light changed and he sailed through. The tires hissed through the puddles. One, two, three, four. For a little while, Bud felt like he wasn't even driving, just rolling along, coasting, automatic, easy. He didn't have to think about it.

The light at the five-way finally caught him. He sat and listened to the wipers drag across the windshield. The red traffic light, the neon beer signs in Tiffy's, blue and red, shone even brighter in the rain.

He took the one-way that bent around to Front Street. The street was empty. Cleve Hardware and Supply was dark; the old man was too cheap for security lights, relying instead on a scruffy shepherd dog. The buildings straggled for two sloping blocks, the roofs pitching and sagging, no two at the same level. Inside them, the floors heaved and buckled, and there were unexpected step-downs, steep inclines. Bud wondered how the dog would even know if there was an intruder, in that wilderness of pipes and commodes, chains and bolts and barrels.

What would a burglar want, anyway? The old man used the night depository and took the next day's cash-drawer money home with him. Tight. He'd made a fortune by measuring each yard of rope twice and never throwing in an extra couple of washers. Too tight to hire help, working his wife and sons like slaves even though there were men enough to hire.

Bud pictured himself weighing pounds of nails. He'd put a few extra in, knowing how the money was hard to come by, knowing too that there was a plain morality in giving more than was strictly accounted for. Roger Cleve wouldn't get to heaven on those pinched pennies, that was certain. But then, he was Presbyterian and surely counted himself among the elect.

There was no light where the street ended at Front. He had to wait. Lot of traffic for a week night.

Just after he turned left onto Front, he saw a hitchhiker. He was wearing a dark poncho, and nothing on his head. His long hair tangled on his shoulders.

Damn, but he looked pathetic. Bud slowed down. Maybe it was a local kid. Looked like someone he knew, but then, in a cold rain who didn't look familiar? He bent his head forward to see if he could recognize him, and the kid took a step off the curb.

No, it wasn't anyone he knew. And besides, he was only going up the Hill, so what was the point? Bud leaned back in his seat and passed the hitcher.

He looked in the rearview mirror and saw the kid flip him the bird.

The anger came up from his gut, hot all the way. He felt it burn in his throat, acid and foul.

It was the way people looked at him. The hippie, the owlish woman under the plastic umbrella, sometimes his own sons. As though he was taking up space. As though he was in the wrong place, all the time.

Sometimes there was a kind of pity mixed in with the contempt – the college kids, that's the way they looked at him, at the other men as they carried their trays of computer cards in their arms, or if it was raining then wrapped in plastic or tucked in their coats like men on the dole carrying away their loaf of charity.

He belched, tasted stomach juices, swallowed. The foul taste wouldn't go away.

Bud turned wide to avoid a familiar pothole, its presence masked by pooling water. He turned on the radio.

" .... martial law in the Philippines, an accident in Branford sends four to local hospitals, and in the weather, more rain. That's the wrap-up at ten past the hour. Now, here's a view from our nation's capital."

The commentator had a rich, rolling voice, a preacher's voice.

"For the first time in seven years, a week has passed in which no American lives were lost in that spreading combat in Indochina which some are calling the Vietnam War.

"But lest we congratulate ourselves on escaping the morass, we should note that thousands of Vietnamese continue to be killed. Our part of the war is the cleaner part now. Our combat is done from the air, high above those steamy jungle swamps and green rice paddies which have sucked down so many young lives.

"While ground troops head home, U.S. bombers pound the Vietnamese mainland…"

Bud punched the selection button, sending the cultivated voice into oblivion. He sorted through rock 'n' roll, sports, country music, more news. He didn't want to hear news tonight. He was tired of news, tired of all the world's woes. He flipped off the radio.

Still, he kept wondering about the pullout. Would it last, or was it just politics, Nixon going for the vote? When the gooks started to get their asses kicked, he figured, Uncle Sam would jump right back in.

"We didn't learn shit from the last one," he said to himself as he turned onto the bridge.

This war wasn't any different from Korea, except that it was sure as hell warmer. Bud remembered the South Korean troops, how you couldn't trust them to stand and fight. Their hearts weren't in it. The South Vietnamese were the same. But the soldiers from the North, they were believers. Them and the Chinese. They came slipping in at night in their sneakers, through the wire, or in battle they would come in waves, not through the wire but over it, men bridging the razor-tipped coils with their bodies and others climbing over the top of them while they were still alive and bleeding.

Christ, you didn't forget those things. Nobody wanted to hear about it, though. Fight and forget, so the next war can be fought. He could remember the World War II vets talking, but it never made much of an impression on him until he found himself carrying a rifle, crawling elbows and belly through cabbage stumps in a frozen Korean field.

It tore him up when his boys came up to draft age and the Vietnam mess was still going on. He couldn't remember the times he wished his sons all were daughters. Then Mike's number was drawn high and he was safe, but Cory had been sure he'd be going. He just seemed to know.

Cory didn't think about dodging. Bud guessed that was because he always made it clear he was proud to have served his country, whether the war was fought for good reasons or not. He'd raised good sons, him and Lola, respectful, patriotic, not like that dirty longhair back there in the rain. Cory had said he thought he'd just volunteer, after Thanksgiving, and see if he couldn't get some training and then use the GI Bill for college. He never said it was to take the burden off him and Lola, though they knew that was part of it, too.

When the talk started that the war would be over, that peace was at hand, they never really believed it.

His stomach hurt, so bad. Maybe he had an ulcer. He kneaded the flesh over his gut and drove his thumb deep into the sore spot.

Bud turned onto the Steel Bridge. The river was just a black band between the hills, flowing down from its forks. Sometimes the streetlights showed the leaves and trash hanging from the bare limbs, still there from the floods. This had been a bad year for floods in West Virginia, first Buffalo Creek, then Agnes. A hot summer, dry ground, then torrents of rain running across the hard earth as if it were pavement.

When he hit River Road, he went left, toward the plant.

He passed the corner of the fence that enclosed the whole extent of the bottle plant. Bud drove slowly, as he always did.

Executive parking. Tennis courts, ball fields, basketball courts for all the contests between departments.

Front office, the flagpole out front with its lanyards empty and swinging. Cafeteria. R&D. Quality control.

Production. The central mold department, where he worked.

There were no lights inside. The outside security lights, paired like apples from a single stem, directed twin pools of light along the walls and the dirty windows and the weeds.

Batch and furnace. Forming. Decorating.

Someone had scrawled FUCK THIS in the dusty windows of the selecting department, one enormous letter to each pane.

He drove past packaging, the waresheds, shipping. He saw the guard shack and the gray form of Max Yost's head, bent over some magazine. The chain-link fence turned in to frame the back entrance, came back out to the street to enclose the employee parking lots.

At the next corner, Bud yanked the car around in a tight curve and drove back.

Max looked up when he stepped to the door of the guard shack, eyebrows raised and his wide lower lip pushed out as though sizing up this visitor. He waved Bud to a folding chair which, from the overlapping dark rings on its seat, apparently served as a table for his coffee cup, and went back to reading Grit.

He was the last of the bottle-plant workers. You couldn't count the office boys and accountants left to tidy up the bones. Whenever anyone or anything died, the damned paper-shufflers had the final say. When the shutdown came, Max Yost was a few weeks shy of getting the early retirement bonus, and as the most senior worker remaining, had been given the job as night watchman until he qualified.

"Real good story in here. Guy started this business with fifty bucks." Max folded the paper carefully to save his place and set it on the floor by his chair. "How's them classes going, anyway?"

Bud shrugged. "Not so bad, I guess. Don't really see the point in it, but as long as they're payin', I'll give it a try."

"Can't teach an old dog new tricks, at least this one, that's what I said. I'm happy doing this until I get my benefits."

"Don't blame you."

Bud stared out the window at the back of the plant. The streetlights over In-Bend just showed along the top of the roof, so that they looked like a string of those white Christmas lights that used to outline the whole plant.

"You headed home, then?"

"Yeah, but there's no hurry. Lola ate already. She'll warm it up for me when I get there."

Max chuckled. "Always did, didn't she?"

Bud couldn't help but grin, restless and miserable as he was. Lola was a hot number when he met her, and she didn't turn to ice like a lot of women did when they got married and had kids. At least, not until recently.

"I had a woman like her waiting at home, I wouldn't sitting here talking with no old man. What made you stop, anyways?"

"Just got to looking at the place as I drove by," he said. He turned away from Max to consider the loading docks, and how the steel doors were decently locked down over the empty spaces, like coins on dead eyes.

"While it's all in one piece, eh?"

"What do you mean?"

Max leaned toward him. The spring in the swivel chair cried out. "It ain't been announced yet to the union, but I heard some of the New York fellas talking. You knew they were taking out some of the machines and selling them. Well, that's not all they're gonna do. They say they can't sell the place 'cause it's too out of date, so once the machines are peddled, then they're gonna auction off the rights to take 'er down for scrap. Iron and steel, firebrick, that'll all bring a price."

"Just going to knock the building in, then?" Bud felt the shudder of the wrecking ball, tasted dust as walls collapsed.

"Yeah, all that brick, and everything," Max said.

"Enough brick to pave from here to Little Washington."

"Pittsburgh, more like. Remember when they put the new conveyor in and had to knock through a wall? Three thick, and an inside wall at that."

"Yeah. Hell of a job, that was."

They nodded over the recollection.

"Speaking of bricks – I see where the pavement broke up on Linden, and the old brick pavement's still there, good as new."

"I sure do remember those brick streets. Was glad t'see 'em pave over top," Max said. "Got those heaves in them, and ruts. Rattle your teeth out."

"The brick held up better'n asphalt."

"S'pose that's true."

Bud looked through the streaked windows of the guard shack. Each part of the roofline was familiar.

"Can I go inside?"

Max leaned back in his chair, folded his hands across his little pot gut. All of a sudden he looked belligerently possessive, like some hillbilly out of the mountain counties, sitting on the porch of his shack.

"I ain't to let anyone in, 'less they have the okay from up top."

"Christ, Max, you said they're gonna knock it down. What's the difference?"

"Who knows? Insurance, maybe."

Bud shook his head. It didn't surprise him. Max always had kept one eye to the foreman and one to the union steward, playing it safe.

"Fine," he said, feeling a little hot. The chair scraped back from his push as he stood.

Max stood, too. He looked up at Bud. His eyes were bloodshot. It couldn't be from drink – all the Yosts were Pentecostal. Must be from reading those magazines, hour after hour, under that bare bulb.

"It's okay, buddy," he said, and reached out to give Max a little thump on the shoulders.

Yost reached down to where a ring of keys was snugged against a flat, round canister on his belt. "Hey, anybody asks me, and I'll tell 'em Bud MacLean give enough to this plant that he ought to get a look around," he said, and pulled the keys out on the retractable cord.

He let Bud in through the shipping clerk's office. At the door to the warehouse, he stopped and shone his flashlight around the enormous space, picking up dusty steel beams and old caution signs, then he turned it off. The area that had been pitch black outside the flashlight beam became real in shades of ash and charcoal.

"You can see enough from the outside lights, but be careful," he said in a hushed voice. "Lotta stuff been moved around."

And Max was gone.

Bud let his eyes get used to the thin light that came through the dirty windows. He walked through the warehouse. Nothing but dust and a few broken pallets and a pile of box flats that had never been assembled. There was no feeling of the people who used to work here. The space was too big; there were no machines or cubicles to suggest their presence.

He made his way back along the production line. His footsteps echoed now, very loud, the strike of his heels and grit of the soles of his shoes on the unswept floor, and he remembered how he had lost the sound of himself in the rain. It must be like that to go blind, or deaf, he thought. You lose the outside world, and with it, part of yourself. Here in the empty plant he was mighty aware of himself.

In Decorating, he bent down to a sparkle on the floor and found a button. The light, dim as it was, picked out trivial things. It was a small crystal button, probably off one of those blouses that had a keyhole opening at the top of the back, and one little button to close the collar. Backasswards, women's clothes were. He rolled it back and forth between his thumb and forefinger, testing the sharpness of the facets.

They always called this the Hen House. Decorating was all women. Packing and Selecting had a lot of women, too, but there were some men and that changed things. He could remember taking the shortcut from the central mold department across the Hen House, and hearing the pitch of laughter rise. The women worked here like women in a kitchen, gossiping, sniping at each other, but getting the work done thriftily and well.

He breathed deep. The smell was gone, a mixture of a dozen perfumes, and paint, and hairspray, and the plastic smell of the decals as they dried onto the glass. There was a faint scent like that of a dustball pried out of the workings of a neglected machine, coagulated machine oil blackened by mildew and dirt.

Max was right – things had been moved around, moved out. Motors were gone, wires left dangling, and a few machine units were gone, too.

He walked to his right, to the windows that looked out on the cullet yard. The only light on that enclosed place came from red warning lights high on the stacks, and what little illumination leaked through the front windows and across the looted interior. Through the dirty windows,

Bud could see only dark mounds.

He bent to the place where a conveyor had gone through the wall, to carry broken glass out to the yard for remelt. They'd just yanked it out, not bothering to cover the hole. The air rested against his face like a wet rag, heavy, motionless.

The yard came clear. The rounded peak of each pile marked the place where conveyor had ended, glass tumbling from the belt as it turned back toward the building, a long running loop. The shards gathered what light they could, on edge or point or curve, a million ghosts of the reflected sunlight that used to blind a man if he looked out there at the day's height, when the sun came over the walls that enclosed the cullet yard.

The door to the central mold department was locked. Bud shook the door. The lock rattled and the metal door whumped back and forth in the frame that was a little too big.

If the plant was so damned out of date, why were the molds worth keeping behind locked doors?

Bud shoved his hands into his pants pockets. His ring of keys jingled against loose change. Car keys, flat metal, and the weight of two brass house keys. He used to have a key to the central mold, others here and there around the plant. He wished he'd kept the one, anyway, for a souvenir. Something held back from a company that numbered every key, every parking space, every piece of athletic equipment provided to its company teams.

Bud kept walking. He stayed toward the outside of the plant, so that he could see better.

Things were both shadowy and distinct, their outlines blending but details picked out as though burnished free of the prevailing dullness. He saw a bearing shine with that heavy gleam of solid steel from ten feet away, but when he got close, he found it was only the bowl of a spoon.

He picked it up. Twin swirls were stamped into the metal, like the curls on the top of a Dairy Queen cone. Must have come out of somebody's lunch pail.

Recollections tumbled like cullet streaming from the end of the conveyor. Lunch pails lined up. Waxed paper as it was unfolded, a dull crunch, or the crisper sound of foil being wadded. Thermos bottles full of coffee, steaming hot at the morning break, lukewarm if there was any left by afternoon.

Patsy Dalessandro.

Patsy had sat at the end of the lunchroom table, that last Friday, spooning pieces of crumbled cherry pie out of a square Tupperware tub. His nervous wife had melted his plastic pie keeper on the kitchen stove the week before, but Patsy had to have pie every day, even folded like that into a box.

He opened his Thermos bottle and poured into the red cap – the milk had soured in his coffee, and Bud could see the curds spin around.

"Hey, Pat." He reached behind Okey Shrock and nudged him on the elbow.

Patsy looked over. He wasn't mad, the way he normally would have been, cussing his old lady out. He just looked confused.

"I got extra, if you don't mind it with canned milk," Bud said.

He swung his legs over the bench, went and took Patsy's cup and tossed the mess into the cleanup sink. He poured him a cup from his own bottle and put it down, nudged it over to where Patsy sat with his head in his hands.

It wasn't a big deal. When the buzzer went off, they all went back to work, just like any other day.

"Damn it all to hell," he whispered.

The plant went under for a lot of reasons. Some of them Bud didn't understand, how the smart boys could ignore problems when they were being paid so much just to be smart. It was a long death, now that you looked back. First the returnable beer bottles went. The old machines couldn't make the new, thin-walled throwaway bottles, so they were shifted to making more returnable pop bottles. Then aluminum cans came in, then plastics. This line went, then that one. They closed a plant in Ohio and brought the work here. They tried the novelty line, but it was too late to break that market, with the imports flooding in from Czechoslovakia, Belgium, even Japan.

He thought about the Datsun that was parked on the street by the factory gate, a yellow dog-turd of a car. Cars, radios, TVs. Christ, what was the difference between a war you won, and a war you gave up on? Korea gained half a useless country, and Vietnam would gain the same, he figured. The wars were getting smaller, meaner, as though Uncle Sam didn't have what it took any more. Now they couldn't even beat a few rice farmers, when 25 years before they won a whole world. And now we're giving it back to the Japs, all nice and packaged in greenbacks.

Bud walked back through the plant, following the stream that once flowed here, from raw material to the rows of bottles upright in their boxes.

A rat startled away from him. It must have been there before, watching him drift by.

Just another goddamn ghost, he thought. The rat skittered ahead, dodging from cover to cover and then was gone through some hole in the wall.

Bud went in a straight line, past his old place, past the giant furnaces heavy-bellied with the melt allowed to cool in them. In selecting, he saw something strange, stranger even than the eviscerated machines, the empty rooms. Four crates were set like chairs in a circle. He approached cautiously. There was something ceremonial in the way three of the crates made the sides of the square, while the fourth one was set askew, as though the side of the square had been kicked out. Or a top pushed open.

Bud walked into the square. A blanket covered one crate.

There was a musty smell, half-sweet, half-foul. He sniffed, turned, and spotted a furry pile like the body of an animal beside a steel pillar. Some of the parts were scattered away, round as the haunches of a squirrel. He looked at it for a long time before he realized it must be human shit, furred with mold.

Too many places set here for kids getting a little nooky. And bums would have picked a more sheltered place on the back side of the plant, a small room where they could have built a stingy fire. Probably kids came here to do dope. He decided that was the other element of the strange smell, the lingering sweet stench of marijuana.

He wondered how they got in. Probably walked right through the gate while Max was being inspired by another tale of American gumption.

He turned inside the square, from half-light to darkness, to half-light to the false dawn of the security lights glowing through the narrow windowed horizon. He saw the letters spaced along the panes, F-U-C-K-T-H-I-S.

Bud felt, or remembered, the bile in his throat.

He kicked a crate out of the way, destroying the magic of the square, and walked to the windows.

Several panes were broken. Glass crunched under his feet. Two-inch road gravels that had been thrown against the windows were scattered on the floor.

Bud rubbed at the corner of the "F," but the film had been baked hard in the summer sun. It would take water to wash the letters away. He moistened his finger and rubbed the letter, smearing its outline.

He bent and picked up a piece of gravel. It was limestone, not river gravel, sharp-edged where it had been smashed from a larger chunk of rock.

He tapped it sharply against the glass where the "F" was marked, and the pane splintered and fell.

Moist air rushed against his face, warmer than the chill inside the building. He watched a new Camaro go by, too fast, and listened to the wide tires on the wet pavement. He wondered if the driver looked at the plant and if he saw, in that moment, a face in the window.

The car was gone. Bud heard, in the silence it left, a metallic clink clink clink.

Clink clink. Clank. Like a workman with a ball-peen hammer, still on the job.

He realized it was the lanyards on the empty flagpole up front.

Bud felt the stone in his hand, the irregular planes of it. He shifted it to the front of his grip. And calmly, meticulously, he knocked every shard of glass from the broken frame.

Then he moved to the next, and the next. Eight panes, each quite empty when he threw the gravel through the last of them.

WHERE HAPPINESS IS EXPECTED

~

You'd of thought someone would have said something, but they just kept on typing, and me standing there like a post.

The newspaper building had a funny smell, like mildew and warm plastic. Finally this guy who was all butt-end from sitting asked if he could help me. Didn't look at my face, just kind of didn't focus. When I asked for the social lady he smirked and pointed to the back of the room.

The woman behind the desk looked like she starved herself, and the light from the computer made her face green. She said, "Can I help you?" twice before I could answer. I gave her the paper where I'd written it out.

She kept smoothing it on her desk, smoothing the wrinkles from the baby's grabbing fingers, more like she was brushing off dirt. One corner of her mouth turned down as she read and she looked like somebody but I couldn't think who. She wanted to know if Krystel's name was spelled right.

"We can't use personal messages, Mrs. Westfal," she said. "We can't use this part, wishing your husband a happy anniversary."

Then something about needing more information, "a regular an-nouncement, like the others you see in the section," she said.

People like that make you feel crappy. The words were plain enough, but by the saying of them you knew what was meant. And I knew where that man was looking when he wouldn't look in my eyes, right down into my halter top.

I didn't know what to do. I just picked up the paper off her desk and left.

~

I bought a newspaper on the way home. It cost a quarter and a dime from the rack in front of the courthouse, and not ' til I got home and sat down to read did I see it was yesterday's paper. And no anniversaries.

FAMILY was on Page Six. There was a big picture of a bride, real bright and a little out of focus. A pool of satin was arranged in front of her feet like something she could fall into.

"Escorted to the altar by her father, the bride wore an off-the-shoulder gown of ivory silk shantung with a cathedral train. Beadwork and pearls adorned the bodice. Her headpiece was created of ivory illusion and a wreath of silk flowers."

There wasn't any mention of lace. I always wondered what the different kinds were, Chantilly and Venetian and the others.

"She carried a cascading bouquet of roses, pink lilies, baby's breath and ivy. The chapel was decorated with gardenias and roses grown by the bridegroom's father."

I was always partial to gardenia sachets, though Russ said they made him think of a funeral parlor. The smell must have been sweeter than anything. Huge bushes of flowers on each side of the altar. Coming down the aisle, the smell would meet you in waves. Enough to make you feel faint when you let go of your father's arm and were standing there on your own, for a little while.

And then leaving the church, the sun would shine, the air so clean like after rain. You'd run through a shower of rice, down all the steps to a white limo where there would be champagne waiting, and happiness would lift you up and up.

Bells start, high in the steeples, getting louder and louder. The birds fly and they are all doves.

I kept reading and came to where the bride was "the daughter of Mr. and Mrs. Herbert Atkinson of Border Creek."

Herbie Atkinson, that son of a bitch. I pushed the paper across the kitchen table and looked out the window at the bare side of the garage.

Atkinson owned the trailer park where we'd rented, right after we got married. Made us sign a year's lease and then he said there were these clauses. No washing of cars. No hanging out of clothes. No this, no that. And you couldn't be so much as a day late on the rent, didn't matter about when checks came or anything. Once he brought the contract and he shoved it in my face. "Right there, 15th of every month." Shaking it in my face and the flimsy metal steps rattling under his feet.

He had a big old mole on his lip. I always thought of cancer. As though you'd get cancer where you did the most damage, and his mouth was the worst of him.

I leaned over to look at his daughter's face but couldn't see much of Herbie in her; maybe she would be all right. Maybe the flowers and the limo and the white dress and all, it would just keep right on, like at the end of a story when the girl marries the less handsome but good-hearted guy after all her troubles and the pages end there.

Somebody yelled.

I turned to see out the screen door to where the kids were playing on their dirt pile. Mickey was perched up on his yellow dump truck, waving a shovel, and here came Krystel all red-faced, stamping toward the house.

"He threw dirt down in my dress," she whined. She pulled the elastic waistband out so that the dirt fell on the linoleum. "I hate him."

"No you don't." I yelled for him and he came, dragging his toes.

"Why'd you throw dirt at your sister?"

He stood stiff, not giving an inch.

"I want you to apologize." Nothing. I took the flyswatter off its nail. "Sorry."

He glared at his sister. "She hid my shovel."

"Ass-hold." Krystel turned right around on her heel to leave.

"You be sorry to your brother," I said, catching her by the wrist.

"Yeah." Mickey crossed his arms on his chest, like his daddy.

"That's enough out of you, too. Say it, Krystel."

"'Pologize." She looked up at me through those long eyelashes, but that didn't work on me like it did on Russ.

"Now git." I swatted the both of them on the rear end and they shrieked and scooted.

Baby Glen, roused up by the noise, fussed and kicked the bars of the crib. I went into the front room and started the mobile around. He sucked at the rest of the bottom of formula, looking cross-eyed at the animals in the air.

Back in the kitchen, I took the Bible down from the top of the cupboard, next to Mom's platter and the nut dish, and pulled out the letter I'd started.

I got the Bible the year I was 12, after I asked my aunt for one. It was black with red edges. My best friend Karen got a white one that spring at her church, which made me want to go there. I did for a little while but they didn't give me any Bible.

A four-leaf clover fell out of the pages and I put it back, beside a blue photograph of Fishermen on the Sea of Galilee.

"Dear Social Lady,"

That's as far as I'd gotten, what with the kids and the dishes and all.

"This is our fifth anniversary."

I still didn't know what I was supposed to put in this. "More information," she said.

I'd seen on the back page of the gas station calendar where the fifth anniversary was supposed to be wood, so that you got gifts made out of wood. That wasn't very glamorous. Radios and kitchen appliances would be better.

But wood was okay. Kind of old-fashioned. Something that could be cut to fit, pegged together and made to hold. Like this patching of holes and nailing over gaps.

"Dear Social Lady,"

I started a new piece, crossing out the other. "This is the fifth anniversary for Russell and Twila Westfal. We have three children ...."

The writing looked small on the paper. The lines were spaced wide apart, for Mickey to be making his alphabets in Head Start. Blue dotted lines were supposed to mark the tops of the small letters but my capitals didn't even reach.

The dogs started howling and I heard the pickup on the curve, the sweep of gravel as Russ turned hard into the driveway.

He'd been promised three weeks of work – work for a full day, every day.

I put the paper away quick and set the Bible back up on the shelf, then I picked up the bottle that had rolled away from Glen where he slept.

Russ stopped by the steps, watching the kids, and as he stood there he tore a leaf off the rosebush. The bush was near eaten up by Japanese beetles anyway but the blossoms came thick.

The ground underneath was white with petals.

It seemed like the longest time 'til he came in. He dropped his lunch pail on the counter. The knotted way he moved said all that needed be said.

He took the pitcher out of the fridge and drank a quart of the kids' red Kool-aid. He looked toward me once, his eyes low like they can get; I stood with the empty bottle in my hands and let him have the first word, if he wanted. Instead, he went back outside and almost that quick was hammering at something in the garage, a steady harsh clang of metal on metal.

"Marry in May and rue the day," was what Mom had said, so we hung on until June. But there was just as many bad days, I imagined, as there would have been.

Russ would go to angry like a grease fire flashing up, smoky and dangerous. He was worse when he wasn't working, because he cared a whole lot more than his brothers about having a job. It shamed him to be like them.

If his anger came back hard at me, well I could move quick most times. I finally learned what my mother never had, which was, there was times to be silent. Even a gentle word could go wrong. I'd just slip away to the bedroom and tell stories to the kids, or go out where the dogs were tied and scratch their ears.

Russ would come around, if I didn't make him angrier by crying after.

No matter how harsh he'd been, in the night he couldn't sleep without me beside him, his legs and hands and chest close against me. Mornings when I wanted to be up and around I had to lay there in bed, or he would feel my spot empty and wake up.

Something fell in the garage, something heavy. I held my breath until I heard him hammering again.

I got out my letter and looked at what I'd written down. There wasn't much.

Maybe it wasn't the right thing to do. Maybe I wasn't saying it right. Mom Westfal would know, but I couldn't well ask her.

I wanted for them all to read it, down in black and white for Russ and his people. His father, who called me bar trash, but would have made a pass if he dared. His brothers. Graffy, Jim. The neighbors.

It was a testimony, real as anything in the newspaper, those stories about people who had big weddings and parties.

As I got another sheet of paper and started to copy my piece over again, I saw the woman's name up in the corner of the society page. Lucille Preston, FAMILY Editor.

"Dear Mrs. Preston," I started. "Please put our anniversary in the paper, Russell and Twila Westfal of Colquitt Creek Road. We're married for five years now. And we are very happy. We have three children, Mickey who is five, Krystel is four and baby Glen. Our anniversary is on June 3rd."

That wouldn't take up an inch of space in the paper. They'd probably put it in that little print you couldn't hardly see.

A picture, that would be the thing.

There were some old pictures in the album but the newer ones were all in a box. I dug through, finding pictures of Russ with a mess of fish, pictures from his family reunion, pictures of the kids sitting on the hood of the car.

I didn't want to give our good portrait from Olan Mills to the newspaper people and have it ruined. We only got the one big one and the little ones were all gone. Russ's was rubbed raw inside the plastic window of his wallet.

Pictures from the Edgerton District Fair. We're standing in front of the Round-Up. I remember the sound as it spun fast, tilting, the riders pressed out against the walls. The ride was big and yellow behind us, like the sun, and we smiled a little for Dave who wanted to snap the picture. Russ was trying to get me to go on it. He'd tried at every carnival all the way back to when we met at the Firemen's Days, but I didn't trust the machinery. What if someone, stumbling drunk, pulled out the thick black snake of electric lines? What would happen to the people when that wheel stopped whirling around – what would happen to those at the top when the pressure failed that kept them in their places?

I put the snapshot back and shuffled through some more. There was one from Christmas of us and the two kids that wasn't bad, though my face was like a marshmallow from water weight.

I wished that I could have a picture of Russ the way he looked now. Working with the sun in his black hair and shining in the sweat of his back, making the blue and red of the Korean dragon even darker where it snaked up his shoulder.

He lifted the truck door off its hinges and set it against the tree. His muscles stood out and there was a little softness above his belt from too much beer – not a gut, just a gentling that made him sweeter than when he was all cord and muscle and knobby spine.

The picture from Christmas would have to do.

~

I knew my way now. As I went down the hall, a man with a camera slammed the door to Photography and walked quickly toward me.

Where's the fire, I wondered, and I must have smiled thinking about it because he smiled back. I ran my fingers through my hair to freshen it and went right in to the News Room.

The same man sat at the same desk. He looked me in the face and didn't recognize me.

I walked right to the thin woman. Lucille Preston – there was a little sign on the corner of her desk.

"Here's that anniversary," I said. The picture fell out of the paper and slid against her folded hands.

She set it to one side, unfolded the paper and read through it at least twice. "We'll have to edit according to our style," she said, marking through the line about how we were happy.

"But I took out what you said, wishing the happy anniversary."

"We have guidelines," she said, her voice cool and perfect. "There is other information we could use. Where were you married?"

"Mount Tabor Church, up in Morriston." She printed it above the crossed-out words.

"The minister?"

I couldn't remember. It was Karen's old church, but her preacher had died and this one was a woman.

"I don't know," I said. "You can't leave in that part I had?"

Lucille Preston closed her eyes.

"It's important to me – to us," I said, then wished I hadn't.

She said again about the guidelines.

I gave up. The black line through "we are very happy" wasn't going to be erased no matter what I said, I could tell that.

And now I recognized her.

She looked like the welfare woman we had when I was little, her downturned mouth, the frown lines. We went to the welfare office every month and Mom would explain to the woman how many bills she had, and how the food stamps didn't last, and why things didn't get better. I would sit on the couch and pull threads through splits in the turquoise vinyl.

It was mostly the voice that was the same, the voice that said there wasn't any argument.

"... Sunday?"

"Excuse me?"

"You did want this printed on Sunday."

"Yes. This next Sunday." I watched her mark the date at the top of the page and set it in a wire basket. "Could you send me back my picture?"

"Do you have a self-addressed, stamped envelope?"

I shook my head.

"You can pick it up here after it's been in," she said.

Then Lucille looked at me. "Or if it's hard for you to get to town, I can go ahead and mail it to you. We're not supposed to, but I will. What's your address?"

Oh, I knew that voice, too. She had won, now she could offer charity.

"I have a car," I told her. "I will come and pick it up."

The Twitchells are on their porch and they wave as I drive past. The people in the new house, working on their perfect lawn, as usual don't look up.

I park the Chevy in the ruts it had set for itself in wet weather. Now in the summer they're filled with powdery dirt that puffs up into my sandals.

The kids are on their swing set and from the garage I hear Russ singing loud and reckless. He'd put the baby's play-pen under the tree, but the shade has moved and Glen is going to get burned sure.

I go around the car for the bag of groceries that gave me a reason for going to town. I take the groceries in, then come back to move the play-pen.

My eye catches something in the grass, another eye. A brown moth wing tilts in the breeze. I bend under the grapevines and pick it up, a wing from one of those big moths that come on still nights and are spread against the wall of the house in the morning.

"Look here, Glenny Glen. See? Pretty?"

I wave it like a tiny fan, feel the colored dust move between my fingers and the wing.

"See the pretty yellow? Yellow and blue."

Glen's mouth goes round as he coos a sound close to "blue."

The colors ring a clear place, a crinkling window like plastic crossed by a thin vein. Looking through it I can still see the shape of the world.

"It looks like an eye." I touch my face below my eye, touch his. He giggles. "Eye. It's not really. Just these colors and the little window."

But I'd seen the moon shine in such an eye and the nighthawk turn from the moth.

Not so hard for any of us to take borrowed light for real.

"We're going to be in the newspaper, Glenny," I whisper. "We're going to be right there with everybody else."

FLESH AND BLOOD

∾

"I seen 'em," Galen Twitchell said, right hand raised in testimony, head turning a bit away. "There's pictures too, Polaroids, a' that beagle-dog carrying a rabbit in its mouth just soft as a setter."

Barry spit a vapid wad of nicotine gum into the Merchants Association planter. He was trying to quit smoking. "Really?"

"That man trained his beagle to bring them rabbits back, not a bit tore up."

"You can't tell from a picture if it's been chewed," Barry said with some assurance. He knew about hounds from a college roommate, an unlikely pre-med student who sharpened his beagles' desire by giving them rabbits to mangle.

"I seen it myself, and they was not one bit tore."

The neighbors stood back under the metal awning of the funeral home, out of most of the drizzle that swept drearily back and forth. Barry thought the old man was lying, putting one over on the townie who had moved out to Colquitt Creek Road, but he wasn't sure enough to call him on it.

They'd left their wives sitting inside, where it was too warm, and come out here where it was too cold but at least clean of the flower smell and strange intimacy of the dead man.

"I don't imagine he provided well for her," Barry said, changing the subject.

The old man chuckled at that.

∾

"That boy never got himself set right to the world," Elva said, her voice murmuring low so it wouldn't carry to the bereaved family sitting in front.

Carol nodded. She looked at the flowers. The florists must have a glut of snapdragons.

When they'd moved last summer into the new split-level beside the Twitchells' farmhouse, she began comparing lawns and gardens along the road: trees in need of pruning, ancient mounds of spirea and forsythia, tractor tires filled with geraniums, lawn swings. A real patchwork. Few of the houses had foundation plantings, anything you could call landscaping.

The yard around the dead man's house was bare except for a tangled rosebush by the steps. He had been mowing with his shirt off, on a Wednesday afternoon; she remembered because she was returning from her pottery class and had just noticed a crescent of clay at the base of a fingernail when she looked up, saw him. She slowed down. It was the first time she'd seen the tattoo on his shoulder.

"What happened?" she asked, prodded by the soft expectancy in Elva's brown eyes.

"Oh, he was the usual kid, a bit wild in high school, not so diff'rent. He went in the Army. Looked real good in that uniform when he come home, but somethin' happened and he was out of the service."

That must have been where he got the tattoo. It covered nearly his whole shoulder with blue and purplish red, something intricate and snaky. She'd slowed down, trying to see what it was. He stopped the mower and stood leaning on the handle, smiling at her, almost laughing. His dark hair curled on his neck and sweat poured off him, staining a yoke on the back of his jeans. She nearly hit the mailman's truck when she speeded up.

He had waved to her each time after that, and she'd nodded as country people did. A short nod that was polite enough, let you keep your hands on the wheel and eyes on the road.

"I heard that he was drinking," she confided into sparse curls.

Elva looked straight ahead into the rows of empty chairs between them and the family who sat all bowed and slumped like end-of summer flowers.

"The paper said as much. It's not surprising. See it with a lot of the young fellas, they leave and come back, thinking there's something for them here and then remembering why they left."

～

"Petey Lange's boy, Fred, he told me the inside of that car was just splattered with blood, like paint," the old man said. "Blood and beer."

That would be the kind of thing Lange would say, surely part of the reason why the childhood bully worked on the emergency squad. Barry felt he had to add something. "They had to cut the door away. I looked at it down at the wrecker service. You can still see one of the beer cans up under the front seat."

Galen smoothed large-knuckled hands across his lapels. It appeared he wanted to hook his thumbs into them like suspenders. "He did a lot of drinking. Him and his whole tribe. Drinking and turkey-fryin' and fighting, and racin' round. You know his brother lost a leg coupla years ago, motorcycle accident."

"He must have been doing 80 around that turn."

"Stupidity. Just stupidity. A local boy like him ought knowed that curve inside and out. Them trees ain't knobbed up like that for no reason."

You were never local enough, Barry thought. He'd lived his whole life in this city, could tell you who owned each one of the businesses that faced them across Commerce Street, and who worked in them. But when he and Carol followed the new expressway out to settle in the northwest corner of the county, you would have thought they'd arrived from California.

He remembered when the brother had his accident by a picture in the newspaper. It was nobody he knew.

"Should be a guardrail there," Barry said.

"Dump truck peeled it up some years back. State never got around to replacing it," Galen said.

～

"Why don't you take off that wrap?"

Carol shook her head. "I must have a chill," she fibbed. Elva's all-purpose polyester dress of blue and purple flowers looked more appropriate than her own black. Carol knew that the hundred little winking buttons down the back were all wrong for this. She pulled the fluffy wrap higher on her shoulders, tried to ignore the heat.

"She looks a lot younger than him," Carol said.

"Nearly 10 years."

He looked no more than 25, though looks could be deceiving. Could the girl be that young? She had to be at least 20, with three kids. Had to be.

"Some families just got bad luck," Elva murmured. "That girl's mother had near the same situation. Husband was killed in the mines when she was young, had a couple a' kids. She took to barmaiding, gone a' nights, and that was hard on them two girls."

"Did she leave them alone?" Carol was horrified.

Elva shrugged. "The older one, she was nine I think. What was she gon'ta do?"

"No wonder she ended up married so young." Carol looked at the child-widow, dandling a baby on her lap. Widows weren't supposed to have bleached hair. "I hope she learned something from her mother's mistakes."

"You don't know what all you'll have to face till you face it," said Elva in her Sunday school voice. "Don't be saying how smooth your road is 'til you see where your ruts tend."

Carol thought of Barry, standing outside with his face blotching like it always did in raw weather, and though it gave her a hollow feeling to think of him dead, she knew she would cope. Sometimes she chastised herself for being morbid, because she would think about being on her own, about how she would learn to handle the heavy gas weedeater, and make sure the septic tank was pumped on schedule.

~

Barry wondered if the old man's black suit was one he'd bought for his own burying. Country people did that. He couldn't imagine opening your closet every day and seeing your funeral clothes hanging there.

Galen had walked over to tell them about the death. They didn't know the man, had been selective in meeting people along Colquitt Creek. The family that lived in the gaunt old place with a lawn cratered by chained dogs wasn't on their list of neighbors. The Twitchells had made it clear they should go to the funeral home anyway. It fell into the category of "something you did."

He felt magnanimous for having offered the old folks a ride. Even if Carol had been the one who thought to ask, he'd done the driving and had held the back door open for her to slide in beside Elva. Galen took the front seat without asking, sitting so straight that his home-barbered gray hair brushed the roof.

"Both families are no-account. She ain't got nobody but a sister. He's got relations to Hell and gone, no lie about that," but Galen paused, nodded to a man walking into the funeral home.

As soon as he was through the door, he continued, " ... not a good'un of that whole tribe."

"Was he in trouble? With the law?" Barry wondered if they should have come here. His boss made it clear even which civic organizations were proper for membership.

"Nah. But he got a dishonorable discharge from the Army, and that ain't easy to do nowadays."

Barry put his hands in the pockets of his topcoat and turned away from the street.

～

The rusty green pickup had been sitting in the funeral home parking lot when they arrived. Carol was surprised. She'd never seen the girl drive, either the truck or the swaybacked old Impala now on display at Stoneking's lot. Somehow she had thought she couldn't.

A man came in by himself. He had a long jaw, a face for sorrow. He went to the widow and bent down to talk with her, and then she stood and walked him over to the casket.

The visitor looked at the dead man's face, set for dignity but not all that different from the department store portrait on a shelf above the casket. He'd been sitting for the picture while she stood, her arms around his shoulders and her hands locked tight across his chest with the tiny diamond carefully displayed. He smiled, showing surprisingly even teeth and the comma of a dimple. She had only smiled a little.

The girl stroked the casket spray of red carnations and fern. The man said something and she nodded, then turned her face away from him and the seated mourners.

"She was from over Cowinton," Elva confided. "They met when he was home on leave. There was the carnival down at the ball field, and that's where they met. Too bad, her being so young."

The marriage, Carol wondered, or the death?

The girl pulled a tissue out of the sleeve of her knit dress, wiped her eyes and blew her nose. The visitor held her shoulder a minute, then sat down by himself at the end of a row.

Her face was white, eyes puffy. She had the kind of sharp face that you never saw without makeup. Naked, the weakness was revealed in the point of her chin and the flat planes of her cheeks.

"That's her sister. She's in from Detroit," Elva said as a woman came in.

She had the same sharp face but her body was thick, from too much work and too much food. She had a toddler on each side of her, not a year apart in age. The boy tried to punch the girl behind his aunt's legs, but she ducked forward and clung to the hem of her skirt, peering at him.

~

"She got herself knocked up right straight," Galen said. "They just keep shelling them out, and him not with a steady job. That kind of people don't care."

"Three kids," Barry reflected.

He and Carol were going to have children, in a few years. They couldn't decide if they wanted one or two. Maybe they'd use gender selection techniques, try for one of each. Might as well.

Even if he died, Carol wouldn't have to struggle. Insurance took care of that. And she had received her history degree when he did his MBA; Carol could go to work any time though probably all she could do would be teach.

"Did they own their house?"

Galen snorted. "That's his, somehow. A brother owns it, or the family owns it, all together. I don't know as she'll stay on there anyways."

"Kind of far out."

"Them's on welfare likes to be close to the office."

"She'll have to get AFDC."

"No reason not to. We're keeping enough of 'em on it."

Barry watched the sign sputter to life at the pizza place across the street. Federico's. An Italian flag was painted in the window. Jim Heller owned it, not a drop of Italian in him but he'd bought it off the original Federico when he couldn't figure out how to charge enough to stay in business.

He saw Galen's eyes, sharpened for farm distance, fix a man as he came out of the hardware, locked the door and turned quickly into the Time-Out Tavern. It must be Howard. Barry never paid that much attention to him at the Rotary meetings.

"She'll hook another one, like him," Galen said. "She's got that switch to her walk."

"Not a bad-looking girl."

"Bit hard."

"Probably she's had to be," Barry said.

"Yeah."

The old man brushed his hands down his suit front again. His mouth worked as though he were sucking on unripe fruit. "He used to knock her around. Put a strap to her fierce, once't I recall. But she's a sassy little thing, liable she deserved it."

Barry thought how childlike she'd looked when they made their brief call inside, all formal with her cold handshake and thank-yous, a pink bra showing through the open knit of her black sweater-dress.

~

The last visitor had been too much. The girl sank into her seat, anchoring herself against the sobs that swelled out of a deep and inconsolable place. A dark-haired woman sitting beside her, maybe her mother-in-law, pulled her face into her chest and let her cry.

"Oh, it's a shame," Elva said.

Carol was embarrassed to feel a hot tightening in her throat, as though she might begin crying, too.

"That poor girl never had a chance. Nor'd he. It was like they was doomed to make their lot twice't as bad as before." Elva knotted her hands in her lap. "Poor and young. Lord, the lambs that ain't nobody gon'ta bring home."

"Maybe she can get into a program, for training." Carol tried to think what a girl with three babies could manage.

Elva shook her head. "Too late," she murmured.

"But she's young."

The older woman gripped Carol by the wrist, her livid fingers showing muscle as well as bone. "Young only makes it the worse. My girl Sissy wasn't much older than she was. Got pregnant from that Tripp boy and Galen, he couldn't understand."

Carol sat very still.

"He locked her out of the house that night, for love of her, he said, and I was scared to let her in. Galen was a hard man then. I crept down late and put out blankets and some food, but in the morning they was where I left 'em. And no word since."

The dark-haired woman patted the widow on the back, gently as if burping a baby.

"I thought she'd find it in her heart to call me, or write a letter some day. Galen, he eased later, but there was no word. And ever' day I think of her, not a day goes by I don't."

The girl sat up and her hair was stuck to her face. She pushed it back, damp and the curl going out. She took a deep breath and sat straight, facing the casket and the picture of her husband that grinned from the gilded shelf.

Carol bit her lip, hard.

She grieved for Elva, and Sissy.

She wondered about being married to a man with a tattoo on his shoulder.

∾

"It isn't natural," Barry said. "Those beagles."

Galen nodded. Barry could almost hear him say, "S'pose not."

"How do you think he trained them?"

"Like bird dogs, setters and the like," Galen answered.

"Setters have a soft mouth by the breeding."

"Most times. The stubborn ones, they fix up a dummy with pins sticking out. Them dogs bite down and feel the hurt and the blood come. They learn quick to be soft-mouthed, I guarantee. Taste a' their own blood, that makes 'em gentle."

BE AN ANGEL

~

Wanda stared at the back of the hotel bar, a wall of glass overlooking a terrace where maybe people sat on some other spring evening. Tonight the weather had closed in, until the only reference point was a traffic light at the corner, bouncing in the driving rain that had packed the convention-goers into the bar.

That's why the windows of roadhouses were painted over, she thought, so you didn't have to stare over the top of your drink into that dark.

Matt came from behind her, leaned close, and when he spoke his breath came out in little bursts that she felt in the hairs on her neck. "You're an angel," he said. "Can I get you something?" She shook her head. He came back with a glass of red wine, took the chair next to hers at this table so small it barely had room for their hands curled around their drinks.

Matt was older than she by some years, trim, his face lean but not yet gaunt. He knew about movies and current books and he liked kayaking and baseball. All she could think, one of those mind-racing things she did at night, the same phrase over and over, was that she had been off the market a long time and she didn't know her book value.

"So, where have you paddled?" she asked. Already she had caught on, learned to say paddled, not kayaked.

"All over. Mostly right around here. What I really like is sea kayaking, going island to island along the Outer Banks."

"Not whitewater?"

"It's okay, I'm just more a touring sort. I like distance more than speed, and the ocean has its own challenges."

Wanda leaned in to hear him against the noise, widening her eyes, attentive, aware of how a dark swath of her hair fell across her cheek. Feeling like a teenager, conspicuously flirting, she settled back in the chair and immediately regretted the distance.

"I canoed once, in Girl Scout camp, but what I really wanted to do was learn to ride horses."

"So do it." Now Matt leaned toward her, sincerity crinkling around his eyes. "Don't wait. Find a stable and sign up for lessons."

Wanda sipped her ginger ale through the narrow red straw.

He was talking about how a man, as he gets older, reevaluates his life, looks to experience all the things he hasn't, sees what is important. "Of course, that makes me sound like an old fart," he added.

Wanda smiled and shook her head.

Matt put his arm across the back of her chair and his hand on her shoulder. He wasn't patting, stroking, really doing anything but exerting a kind of pressure that made it natural for her to lean toward him. It felt a little strange, a little wonderful. Whatever aftershave he used was neither sweet nor, thank heavens, fatherly.

A woman she'd met at the Friday afternoon icebreaker, Helen something, came into the bar and looked around for a seat. She glanced at Wanda, raised her hand with a flash of rings and bracelets, and began winding her way through the crowd of school administrators, consultants, salesmen. As she got closer, Wanda realized that she wasn't looking at her but at Matt.

"Hi! God, this place is jammed. Do they ever build a convention hotel with a bar big enough for conventions?" Her voice was big, brassy. She wore oversize glasses and too much eyeliner.

"Good to see you," Matt said, standing. Wanda felt a cold place where his arm had been. She stood as well and offered her hand.

"We met at the coffee urn," she said. "Wanda."

"Oh, honey, of course I remember you. From Covington, right?" And the woman reached both arms across the table and gave her a hug. "How are you enjoying the program?"

"These things are pretty much alike, but there's always something to learn," Wanda said.

Matt scouted out another chair from a table where all the men were standing to see the game on TV. "May I get you something to drink?"

he asked, with the slightly overwrought gallantry that had first attracted Wanda.

"Sure," Helen said.

"And what do you have there?"

Wanda looked at her glass. "Yes, please. Ginger ale."

Matt nodded, but his lips moved forward in an appraising way. Wanda could almost see him weighing what her choice signified – abstention, recovery? – but she offered no explanation.

"What's that you're having – Cabernet? Great," the other woman said to Matt, and Wanda felt a subtle point being lost on one side, gained on the other.

"I always think I'm gonna get tired of these dos, but then I sign up and here I am, big as life," Helen said. She turned to Wanda. "And you get to know people over the years. You haven't been at the spring show?"

"No. I just moved here a year ago."

They watched the crowd. Matt connected with the bartender and came back carrying the drinks, with coasters tucked under one thumb. He put them down and centered the glasses on them. Wanda smiled at that.

"You never get over being a waiter," he said.

"In college?" Wanda asked.

"And after. I started a business on my own and fell flat, didn't want to go back to Dad and the family business. I was getting my finances back in shape when he had a heart attack and I came home. Never to leave again, amen."

"Well, your booth sure looks good these days," Helen cut in. "I remember last year you didn't have the video thing."

"It helps," he said.

"I saw where Steve McKenzie had three spaces reserved, but when…"

Wanda tuned her out. She watched the lights and blurry reflections swelling on the glass wall, people circling, socializing, and she felt like the odd-out, again. In the two years since Allen left, she'd worked on herself, her career, her money skills, and only now was she ready to relearn the habits of courtship. The convention was her coming-out party, in a way, and hadn't been going badly until this woman showed up.

She had met Matt in the vendor area, just as it opened that morning. He had his promo loop running and brochures fanned on the table while many of the other booths were dark, their keepers straggling in from late nights and late breakfasts.

"Matthew Pike," she said, as she added a Pike & Co. mousepad to her bag. "Founder and sole proprietor?"

"My father, actually. I go by Matt–the other sounds too – apostolic."

She opened a brochure and studied it, well aware of the man with the slightly overlong hair–but an honest gray – and no wedding ring. He complimented the scarf she was wearing. She picked up a pen. Shameless, she said, gathering up goodies to be divvied up around the office when she got back. Take two, he said.

Wanda found herself near his booth that afternoon, killing time until the call came for dinner, and they found themselves walking together, and taking seats at one of the huge round tables where no one could reach anything in the center and the meal was a long process of handing around the trays and baskets and cruets.

She flirted, emboldened by the good humor at the table, but she was never unaware of her motions, her words. She sat straight, haunted by a round-shouldered image of herself from ninth-grade posture training.

Matt, for his part, was an agreeable dinner companion. He focused on her, talked about films, disagreed mildly about Kubrick and then shifted the conversation smoothly to his sports interests, running and paddling and sailing. He was a bit obvious about his fitness, she thought, but she played along. And when the speaker was introduced, he backed his chair around to see the head table, and it seemed, to get close to her.

At the end of the program, he took her hand, squeezed it, and asked if she would like to meet for a drink.

And here I am, she observed, sitting back while he leaned toward Helen, even taking her bangled wrist to demonstrate the proper method of checking a pulse.

They must be old lovers, Wanda thought, and flushed with anger. This woman was a Shelley Winters sort, aging from ripe to overripe, not all that attractive but lots of energy. She could feel herself fading in the sizzle of that high voltage, taking up less and less space with her plain haircut and bare wrists.

He's too old, she reminded herself. Too liberal. Too obviously on the make.

It didn't matter. She leaned into the conversation, touched Matt lightly on the arm to make a point. He turned toward her, that brilliant cinematic smile, the lines cutting deep to frame his mouth.

"I went to London last year, my first time. For the theater season …"

"Did you see that ABBA thing?" Helen cut in. "The one with all their songs? Or what is that play that's been running forever?"

"The Mousetrap," Matt said.

"You could get caught up in that," she said, laughing, too loud.

"I've seen it," he said. "It's a fusty old mystery but it just goes on and on. Habit, I guess."

"There's nothing like a good bad habit," Helen said, nudging Matt but looking at Wanda.

Anything he might have said was drowned in the cheering from the football group. Most of the men were raising their arms, shouting, while those on the losing side groaned and covered their faces. It was impossible to see the score from here, just figures scurrying across a too-green field.

Wanda saw Matt catch Helen's eye, then look away, look back to her. She was suddenly irritated with them both, took a long sip of her drink and thought about slipping away.

But it was Matt who made the first move, checking his watch and standing up abruptly.

"My apologies, ladies, but my alarm rings at 5 a.m."

Wanda felt a small jolt. He bent toward her, it had been nice, hoped he would see her again, he had his schedule and his miles to put in come morning.

She felt what wasn't being asked, close as he was, his hand drifting across her shoulder. But Helen sat there blinking like an owl behind her glasses, and as he began to walk away, Wanda couldn't bring herself to call after him, slip him her room number. He turned left toward the elevators and was gone.

Wanda flicked at the straw in her empty glass. It spun around the inside of the rim, settled pointing back toward her.

"He's married, you know."

Wanda flushed, ashamed at being caught out.

"I knew," she said. The dropped "we" at dinner, the fastidious avoidance of certain topics that she recognized but had chosen to ignore.

Helen was looking at her, and Wanda expected some kind of judgment, but was surprised at the great kindness she saw instead.

"Matt and I go way back, honey. I don't suppose he's an evil person, just got himself caught. He married a woman with some money, back when he was in financial trouble. I hear he stays in town and she stays on their farm – she's big into horses."

Find a stable. I guess he'd know something about that, Wanda thought.

She considered going to bed, but didn't want to follow Matt to the elevators just yet. She glanced at the TV, now on basketball, and thought about her room, watching Headline News and then the Weather Channel until the music and whirl of storm systems lulled her to sleep.

A waiter came by, collecting empty glasses. He asked if they needed anything.

"Ginger ale," Wanda said.

Helen nodded. "That's a good choice. One late-night glass of wine is nice, two is telling your brain to take a vacation."

"I'm not much of a drinker. I guess it shows," she said, almost as sharply as she felt. Who was this, her mother?

"Nothing wrong with that. I just like a glass of wine to wind down with. Everyone says I'm on overdrive. Turn down the voltage, Helen old girl, that's what they say."

Wanda laughed, couldn't help herself. "I guess I'm just on edge," she said.

And then it came seeping out, like water finding its way through the crevices of a dam. Allen's infidelity, revealed in the process of the divorce. The shame of it. The shame of her singleness after 20 years, how hard it was to be 40 and alone.

"I just can't do the bar thing," Wanda said. "I can see the men sizing me up, how old is she, how crazy is she, maybe a manhater, a clinging vine . . ."

"It must be tough. You're used to having someone there, and all of a sudden, he's gone."

"The only breathing thing in the house is my cat, and I wouldn't know he's there except he's old and he snores a little." Helen laughed along.

Wanda felt such empathy, such understanding, then noticed for the first time the thin gold band lost among the costume jewelry on Helen's hands.

"You're not single."

"No, I'm married."

Figures, Wanda thought. Pity the poor single woman, but keep her away from my man.

"I've been married 28 years. I met Jim just before he shipped out – he'd joined the Marines. He came by the Dairy Kone for a milkshake, and we started talking. Lord, he was a cute one, and I fell head over heels even though he was just a pup right out of high school."

Before Wanda could make her escape from the litany of a perfect married life, Helen started again, and her tone shifted.

"He said he wasn't good at expressing things, and I took that for the way a man loves. I was wrong. We got hitched over in Elkton, Maryland. He was in training two weeks later, and then posted to a carrier. He used to write me a lot, all about the Corps and his squad. He made it a career, a career out of volunteering for shipboard duty and foreign postings."

Wanda looked at Helen, past the reflective lenses into brown eyes filled year by year with sorrow, like leaves thickening in a forest pool.

"Did you have kids?"

Helen nodded. "Three."

"Allen and I couldn't."

"They're all on their own now. All over the country, the furthest one got all the way to Alaska. Course they were raised all over. Mostly it was just me and them. He was stateside for one tour and that was the toughest one, him hard on the kids, and they were heading into their teens by then."

"And you're still with him?"

"I signed on for that," Helen said. "When he retired, I thought things might get better. And then Jim was diagnosed with stomach cancer. And you gotta stick."

"I'm sorry."

Helen reached over and patted her hand. "Oh, honey, that's just the way things work out. We all get our bag of troubles to carry, and I guess I'd as soon carry mine. Look at poor Matt, now. And you've been treated shabby."

Wanda looked down. Her hands lay loose on the table. The mark where her engagement and wedding rings had been, the rings she had worn for a year after he left, was gone. She felt a little embarrassed at her earlier complaint.

At least there had been a time, Wanda thought, a time when we had passion and joy. At least we had love once, not just an obligation.

"He's been in and out of the VA for surgeries, the cancer spreading once they cut him open and the air got to it. That last time, he had a stroke." Helen seemed to take a deep breath. "I promised him I wouldn't put him in the home, but I tell you, I thought I was through with diapers 20 years ago."

"He doesn't know what he's missed, not loving you," Wanda said.

Helen shrugged, which sent a ripple through her earrings and necklaces and bracelets.

"Like I said, we get what we get. I take care of myself. Like this convention, this is my vacation. Get to eat out, talk with folks."

"Are your kids with him, while you're gone?"

Helen laughed. "Oh, no. They scarce remember to send him a pair of socks for Christmas. I get a respite worker to come in, even if it does make the old man mad to have some other woman handling him."

She wanted to ask, didn't you ever think about running away? Didn't that loneliness scare you into looking at another man who might have brought you happiness?

Wanda glimpsed something of what must have sent Allen running, running blind, not running toward anything but running away from the gaping hole that somehow had opened between them. She remembered the girl in the linen dress with flowers woven in her hair, walking toward Allen at the altar, him with a borrowed suit hanging on his skinny frame. It seemed like she had floated up the aisle. Both those people were long gone, changed year by year into strangers, bound together by the routine that had grown up between husband and wife.

The bar was nearly empty, the wait staff hoisting chairs on the four-tops at the back, the kitchen help carrying out racks of glasses to set up for the next day.

"I think it's time," Wanda said.

"You sure are right about that." Helen seemed to shut down, her energy folding in on itself.

They took the elevator upstairs in silence, the warmth between them cooling as soon as the doors closed behind them. They observed the standard etiquette of body space, eyes fixed on the numbers lighting one after another.

Helen got off first. Just as the elevator settled at her floor, she threw open her arms and gave Wanda another of those intense, unexpected hugs. "You're going to be all right, now," she said. As she stepped into the hallway, she turned and raised her hand, a wave, a benediction. The bronze doors slid shut with a ping, and Wanda felt the weight on her aching feet as the car rose.

Wanda's room was too cool, the air conditioning pumping through the vents. She turned the thermostat up and got undressed.

She slid off the expensive pantyhose, thin as a breath, and put them in the side pocket of the suitcase. She rolled up the lacy matched underwear and stuffed it in the dirties bag.

Instead of the new nightgown, elegant cream satin, she put on a soft old T-shirt, turned back the stiff comforter and chilly sheets, and climbed into the king bed.

I was that close, she thought. That close to sleeping with a total stranger.

She should be restless with desire, as she had been when Matt first touched the small of her back, pressing against her as they presented their tickets at the door to the banquet room. "Be an angel and sit with me," he said. And then after dinner, he said he would see her in the lounge, and when he headed toward the elevators she thought, oh, he's going to check his room, to get condoms, to prepare.

Maybe this was the way to stop seeing Allen's face, she had thought.

But as she turned off the lamp and the room settled itself into the grays allowed by the streetlight glow seeping past the curtains, she realized that what was going to erase his image was not that thin face, that soon-to-be-forgotten Matt, that mirage, but this long hard staring straight up into the dark.

WESTGATE

~

GARY NURSED THE ACCELERATOR, feeling for a miss, a click, a cough. The engine lub-dubbed like a delicate heart, hot fluids pumping sluggishly through the block, worn belts glazing on their pulleys.

He goosed the Pontiac through the caution light. It was hot and he wanted to get to Westgate. He was eager for the movie's blue glow that hushed everything: kids fighting in the back seat, brakes squealing toward their rivets, sun hammering under the tinted band at the top of the window.

Angela was already in silent mode. She leaned away from him, hands crossed on her big black pocketbook. Her sandal tapped against the door panel. She was mad before, about the cost of the alternator, and mad again when he asked the kids if they wanted to see a movie.

But she wasn't the one who laid on her back under the car when the water pump went. She wasn't the one busting her knuckles to change the oil. She wasn't the one who knew that a junkyard alternator might leave him halfway between work and home after midnight.

A fight just to keep the car running.

Gary swung left to get to High Street and came down the side of the plaza where the two-dollar cinemas were. The argument in the back seat had tightened to the ugly close-quarters battle of hissing and pinching; it was beyond the choice of movies, now, to old grudges, terrible threats.

The kids had been excited, at first, calling to see what was playing, immediately unable to agree. The girl was just enough older that she wanted to see the romantic comedy, while the boy wanted the children's movie.

"We'll let your father decide," Angela said. "Like he does everything."

Her pink lips were pressed together. She ran her fingers through the short curls on the back of her neck, over and over like she was calming herself. So that was that.

He guessed they'd see the cartoon. It didn't matter. What was the point of those romantic things, for the girl to drink that in, movie after movie? To see the hero pull the heroine at last to safety, with just one hand to drag her out of danger. Now what that really felt like, he sure could tell her. Lashed to her, his wrist breaking but unable to let go, the weight of the marriage like iron, the hard unyielding pull. And no escape, not like in the movies where the injured hero had the strength to lift the girl over the edge, up the elevator shaft. He was never pulled over the cliff by her kicking weight.

Gary slowed by the Biscuit World where he sometimes got breakfast, turned left into the strip mall. Not a single operating business at this end. Too much crime now, holdups, gangs spraying their marks all over the buildings like dogs. The springs squeaked over broken speed bumps. They passed a boarded-up Hills and an empty furniture store, then the Goodwill, what used to be a Mexican restaurant, a discount drug store and three-screen cinema. The marquee was empty, except for ALL SEATS TWO BUCKS. Tan stucco peeled along the false roofline.

The kids had settled down or given up. They slumped in the back. He knew they hated the mildew smell in the movie theater, the tattered seats, the stale popcorn poured out of bags. But mall cinemas charged three times as much; with everything falling apart, you did the best you could. You spent the money where it had to be spent, on things that needed it worst and would last the longest, and economized elsewhere. He couldn't remember ever going to a movie with his mom and dad. He should tell them that when they started that eye-rolling.

He shut off the car and sat with his hands on the wheel, listening to the tick of the engine.

"You suppose it'll start when we come out?" she asked.

"Yeah, she'll start." He'd done everything he could, checked the ignition system, cleaned the battery terminals. The crusted residue was yellow, greenish, and he had to scrub it away with baking soda. Nasty festering stuff. Hard to believe something mechanical could do that, more like a body, phlegm and mucus and pus, infection. He scoured the terminals with a brush then scrubbed his hands. They tingled afterward, from the acid or the scrubbing.

~

The kids were yanking on the door handles when he told them to simmer down, they had to run in to the drug store first. The girl sighed and threw herself back against the seat. "At least don't get the outdated stuff," she said.

"OK." He leaned through the window. "What do you want?"

The girl shrugged. "Good 'n Plentys," the boy said, right away, smart enough to go for what he wanted.

The sun was just overhead, sending little shadows ahead of them as they walked to the store. Nothing else moved on a Sunday afternoon, the parking lot almost empty, only a pair of crows flapping toward the ragged pine trees.

Angela took herself off to the candy aisle by way of cosmetics. Gary wandered over by the magazines. Stroke books, car magazines, muscle magazines. Computers. He finally found an outdoor magazine and paged through it. Oversized bucks, their antlers too large, their heads held up for photos by bearded hunters. Lots of snow, the page glistening, like Russia. On the next page, the desert.

She came up beside him. She had paid for a jumbo box of Good 'n Plentys and some kind of cheap chocolates and was taking them out of the plastic bag and stuffing them deep inside her black purse. He liked how that made her look larcenous.

Angela hung the pocketbook back on her shoulder. He remembered when there was softness to her, her shoulder padded and pink. She was all bone now, like her hands. Gary thought that, in the middle of the movie when she became absorbed in the plot, he would let his hand drift over and take hers.

He went back to the counter to get his cigarettes – she wouldn't pay for his filthy habit. The rabbity clerk wore a striped tunic, her lip gloss whitening on her chewed lips.

"I hate this," Angela whispered. "Sneaking candy into the movies."

"Marlboros. Hundreds," he said to the clerk.

The girl turned and studied the rack of cigarettes, one hand raised, the other drumming on her thigh, before reaching to get a pack.

He asked for matches, and she looked at him as though there was something odd about that, then bent stiffly and scrabbled around in the shelves.

Angela hoisted her pocketbook; the Good 'n Plenty sounded like marbles. She bent close to him.

"What if they hear that?" she hissed in his ear.

"Okay, okay."

The clerk stayed below the counter.

"What if it rattles?"

"So don't fucking move."

How hard could it be to find some damn matches? The clerk wasn't even looking. He was about ready to tell her to forget it.

When she stood up, she held a gun in both hands. Big. Chrome.

Gary backed up a step.

"Bill! Bill!" The clerk screamed toward the back of the store. "Call the cops!"

Angela whimpered and he turned his head, saw her hands in the air, started to raise his own.

"Don't move!" she said, her voice yodeling up and down. She lifted the pistol. Gary felt a prickling like someone might tackle him from behind. He started to turn and she shrieked, "Don't move!"

"I didn't mean that," he protested.

"Not like last time," she said. Her teeth protruded. "Bill!" she screamed.

"Hey, I don't …"

"Shut up!" she screamed.

Angela didn't say anything. The gun, which had wavered between them, settled on him. The clerk had bitten her lip and a thick drop of blood stood out, like a bead.

Gary felt exposed, sweating armpits, soft stomach. The gun was big, slab-sided, shiny like a toy. It sagged in her grip.

He started to say something, his hands turning out as he explained. The girl's hand jerked. The noise was impossible, too loud, like in theaters with big speakers that made the explosion painful. A billet of steel drove him to the floor, heat roaring through his chest. Too big, too loud, a hole blown in the pipes, noise and heat.

Gary lay with one arm out, the other on the soft of his gut just under the wound. He looked into the fins of the light fixtures. Light poured over Angela's shoulders. She will kneel and cradle my head in her lap, he thought, and tell me she loves me. She has to do that. But Angela just stared, holding onto her pocketbook with both hands, a huge black bird she was keeping still.

MAY APPLE

~

DINA HOLDS THE BEROL PENCIL with the intensity of a child, as though it's too bulky for the narrow, soft spaces between her fingers.

Gerard aches to open her hand, let the pencil roll and fall away from the flatness of her palm, then gently fold her fingers around that turquoise center as naturally as petals cupping themselves at dusk.

Instead, he shifts the pencil in his own hand, significantly, hoping that she will see.

The light is good. It rained during the night, and now the light is washed and green, diffused by the new leaves.

"You don't have to draw every detail," he suggests. "Try just shading that area."

Dina looks over her shoulder at him. He winces at the pose; hair smoothed back in a clip, her head neat and round as a cat's, her nose oddly upturned at this angle. It's too much like an ad he worked on six months ago, an image adapted from an image, blonde perkiness a daydream inversion of his wife's workaday face.

"How do I know what parts to draw in and what to leave out?"

Gerard smiles helpfully. "Just try it." She waits for more, for a literal answer, makes a little mouth as she returns to her newsprint sketch pad.

Last week he'd seen a yellow flower in this patch of rich woods, blossoms gleaming like fairy gold just before it winks from treasure into dead leaves. And about as permanent. All that remains is the deeply cut foliage and the start of seed pods, and the name that Kay gave him, celandine, for the wilted flowers he brought back to their apartment.

The cutleaf toothwort that he draws instead is pretty, the name inelegant for such dainty windblown flowers, but Gerard is angry with himself.

Tuesday, I did the laundry.

Wednesday, Dina came over with the candy bars.

I should have come up Thursday, he thinks, and a line thickens, makes itself deep on the paper.

He knows the toothwort by name because he has drawn it before. Like the celandine poppy it has four petals, but these are small, pale, the whole plant fluttery. Something to catch a woman's eye. Maybe he could work a deal to have this printed up on note cards.

But his eye is drawn, over and over, to the patch of may apple higher on the bank. He begins to sketch the extravagant umbrellas, coarse and familiar, demanding color for the heavy green of the leaves, their lemony juncture with pale green stems stippled red. Demanding the use of oils. Not something that, quite cynically, he could polish off for some quick cash.

He sees that Dina has shaded in a considerable portion of her drawing. It's muddy, the shading as excruciatingly careful as the lines that confine each shape.

But the naive posture of her hand entrances him. He feels the balance of the pencil between his fingers, how it shifts along the plane of his thumb and rides against the callus of his middle finger.

∼

"God, I'm sorry."

A slender young woman stood in the hallway, holding a box of candy bars in one hand, her purse dangling by its cracked plastic strap from the other.

"I didn't mean to interrupt." She switched the purse to her other hand and gestured upward, letting something fly, her eyes rolling to follow. "Just pretend like I didn't ever ..."

Gerard stopped trying to read the printing on the box. Something-something Fund Raising.

"It's no big deal," he insisted. "I'm sure I can find some change. Come in and sit down – I might have to check the chair cushions."

She followed, pushing the door half shut with her heel, then stopped.

His easel stood in the middle of the living room, for lack of space elsewhere, a partially finished watercolor presiding over the paints shut up in their box, the dry brushes. A jar of flowers was centered on a tatted doily on top of the television.

"That's so pretty," she said, not gushing, more as though she were embarrassed to have caught the drawing in mid-stage. "I'm really sorry. Craig's only in kindergarten and they have them selling stuff already. I think it's for curtains, or a projector, or something. Oh, sorry – I'm Dina Morgan, from the other building."

"Nice to meet you. Gerard Dillow."

She set the box on the floor and walked over to the flowers, looked at them closely. "We just moved in. Craig and me. Pete's in the service and ..."

Gerard glanced at her as he dug through the contents of a Mexican bowl – old keys, matches, rubber bands, a spool of black thread with a needle thrust into its side, a "Re-elect Carter" button that had been pressed upon him outside the Foodland, raffle tickets – all those things were there, all the usual, except for the usual loose change.

"I'm babbling. Sorry. God, you let someone sell you some candy bars and she tells you her life story." She walked back to the easel, leaned close, touched the paper lightly with the tip of her finger.

"It's done?"

"I haven't been working on it this morning," he said, as he reached for the odds and ends basket on top of the refrigerator. Surely Kay hadn't cleaned out all the quarters and dimes for the machines at work. "I've been sketching."

She spotted the black-bound sketch book and opened it. Like shuffled cels of an animation, the drawings seemed to leap to erratic life as she flipped the pages. An illusion of movement there, and there – leaves turning, a plant leaping rootless from the ground.

"You're a real artist."

"Art Institute, Class of 1974." He laughed, caught between the self-doubt that clenched itself onto every line and the warmth he felt at her acknowledgment.

"I'm sorry. This is all I can find." He held out two quarters. "Is that enough?"

"Sure is." Dina opened the box. "Almond, crispy or plain?"

"Almond."

She dropped the coins inside the box and they slid between the stacked candy bars to the bottom.

"Well, thanks." Her eyes lingered on the half-finished watercolor.

"Do you paint?" he asked.

"Oh, no! I mean, back in school I used to like art class," she said, and made it sound as if that were centuries ago. Gerard thought she might be 22, 23. She became coltish in her confusion. "I just think, you know, it's so cool that you can do that. Be an artist. I'd love to watch sometime."

He realized, as she quickly turned red, that she wore a saddle of faint, faint freckles across her nose and cheeks.

"No time like the present," Gerard said.

He took the sketchbook, turned to a new page and began, roughing in the bouquet of wildflowers in the pint jar.

Kay had picked those flowers on the lower slopes of the ravine-cut hill, so steep that no one had built there even in the Mon Valley's good years, his Dad's young years – during the war when the blast furnaces and wire mills had roared around the clock. She arranged them in the jar, balancing color and size. He'd pulled them out, after she left for the day, and stuck them back loosely, a more ragged, less controlled look.

"I did used to want to be an artist," Dina said.

"Really?" He struggled with the raised lettering on the jar, the flowing script pressed in glass.

"I got A's in art and I really thought, maybe. But you have to be really, really good."

"Maybe you were."

She made one of those whole-body movements, an eloquent lift of her hands, a shrug that settled in resignation. "Business college. I work at the courthouse, back in the deed room."

"You like it?" He widened the petals of the buttercup, insinuated their cupping curve.

"It's okay. The pay's not great, but the benefits are. Do you work or what? Oh, God, that was all wrong! I mean, do you just do art?"

"When I can." An old working-class shame cramped his wrist.

"Do you teach?" she asked, her voice rising with hope.

"I have. Mostly I freelance for ad agencies, department stores, that kind of thing. It's kind of iffy, but Kay works."

"Does she have dark hair, flipped up?" Dina showed what she meant.

"Yeah."

He doodled with the fine pattern of the doily, beige cotton threads twisted into lace by Kay's grandmother. Fussy. Not like Kay. She was plain, like that hairstyle – he didn't care for it, had liked it better when she wore her hair long and loose. When she was Dina's age – what, seven, eight years ago – when they were dating.

"She's really pretty. I've seen her in the mornings when I'm getting Craig ready. She's a nurse, right?"

"Um-hmmm."

Dina leaned close, watching as he added details, smudging a shadow with the pad of his forefinger. She didn't seem to have anything to say, now. He was aware of the sound the pencil made on the soft texture of the page.

The drawing wasn't bad – better than anything he'd done all week, maybe because of the distraction from his own circling thoughts – but it wasn't good either. Just adequate.

Pretty. It was pretty.

It was illustration, he admitted. Not art.

Gerard had always wanted to go west, fill huge canvases with wide skies and stark stone, the grasses of the Plains bending under a ceaseless wind. Here he felt oppressed by the closeness of the buildings, ugly brick piles like this one, or uglier wood frame houses, gaunt and soot-streaked. The hills came down steeply to the turbid river and all the time the air was damp, close, close.

But if he left, his mother would be alone. He wasn't sure if it was her need that held him, unspoken need, unadmitted, or if he had some clenching addiction of native flesh to the mill town's astringent water and caustic air.

"That could be in a magazine," Dina said.

He smiled, worked the side of the lead down on the edge of the page, then set the flat side against the paper and began to shade, adding depth and weight to the contour line drawings.

"Even an art gallery," she offered, as though she realized she had somehow offended him.

The flowers became dark, shadowed, bruised. Heavy.

Maybe he should take some regular job, whether Kay agreed or not. She made most of the money, and he could have accepted her deciding how it was to be spent better than he could her acquiescence to his decisions. She let him make the budget, pay the bills, and somehow that tightened her control.

Gerard remembered his mother asking him, when he was still a boy and she worked to support the family after Dad's death, what he thought about buying on time. She was a small woman but relentless, in constant motion behind the diner's steel counter, but still she needed a man to tell her it was all right to buy a chair.

An image of his father: he was walking home from the mill, his heavy body and his lunch bucket and thermos outlined in late-afternoon light, red as the mill dust that flew from his shaken clothes.

Gerard ripped the drawing from the book and crumpled it, tossed it into the kitchen.

Dina's sigh rolled with it, an unfolding of dismay.

∼

While some of the may apples are already in bloom, the waxy white flowers pendant from the joint of two leaves, a few are still sprouting through the gray soil. They come up exactly like an umbrella, the top a tough button to jab through the soil, the leaves tightly rolled around the stem.

Gerard feels the easiness return to his hand, the life come back, tingling like blood after a constriction is released.

He works rapidly. The drawing unfurls itself like a new shoot, demanding space, demanding light.

"Gerard."

Startled, he moves, loses his footing and slides a little way down the slope, ending up level with Dina.

She holds a may apple in her left hand, actually, the remains of one.

Both leaves have been broken off and discarded. The flower nods between the stumps. One of its six petals is gone, too.

"Look."

One by one, she presses on the remaining petals, and they break off with a faint, crisp sound. She gathers them into her hand.

The bare apparatus of the flower remains – a dozen creamy anthers around the fat yellow-green ovary which will swell into fruit. It is topped with a sticky mass, unpleasantly similar to exposed brain tissue.

She is awed, or frightened, her mouth slightly rounded – like a child halfway between crying and laughing, or laughing and crying.

Gerard takes the stalk, sniffs, but none of the gardenia-like scent remains.

She opens her hand. Her nostrils tighten as she smells the broken petals. "Hey! They still smell."

Dina extends her hand and he moves as though to kiss the soft tyranny of her palm, wealthy with destruction and green with its aroma.

$\sim$

Gerard and Kay are climbing up the wooded hillside, away from the city and the heat and the thickened air shimmering among the buildings, as if the flood-prone river had come up out of its banks into the valley.

The mills are on July shutdown, quenched, joining the permanent rusty silence of so many along the river.

He tries to hide his laboring breaths. Kay climbs without difficulty. She speaks occasionally but firmly, like a tour guide, pointing out a blue damselfly, the shell of a cicada where it had climbed a stem to molt.

"A deer bedded here," she says, and he nods. The grass is pressed down in an oval space that looks too small for a deer. It looks like a dog's bed.

Then they are in the place where the may apples bloomed. The leaves droop.

Kay turns them over, finding the yellowish fruit. She picks two and hands one to him.

"Here, Adam, it can't hurt you."

He takes it between his thumb and forefinger, remembering tales that it was a tonic to heal all, that it was a poison by degrees.

"Is it safe?"

"Don't trust a country girl?" She nibbles at her fruit. "I used to eat these all the time."

One side of her mouth curls higher than the other as she smiles, a rueful look.

Gerard stands outside himself, an artist considering his self-portrait. A soft man, with thinning sandy hair and weak shoulders. A man without distinction. Softening from within around the lie in his flesh, like poison in the fruit.

He bites into the may apple, trembling with fatigue or his own recklessness. The taste is wild, astringent, spicy, with an overtone of carrion – at once sweet and bitter, hidden, to be found out.

LEARNING TO DRAW WITH PERSPECTIVE

~

GERARD WOKE UP thinking he was home.

Red brick walls curved toward each other above the street like the shoulders of a broken arch, an illusion of molded window glass and speed. The sky was unexpectedly dark.

Kay's foot shifted to the brake and he lurched forward, drawn by his body's inertia as the car slowed. He looked toward his wife and everything dropped into focus.

"What time is it?"

"Seven o'clock," she said, her face still tilted forward, watching for the green. "You've had a nice nap."

It had been late afternoon when he fell asleep, the sky a hazy gray. He remembered half waking when they left the interstate. The sky was far too dark. They must be driving into rain.

"Sorry," he answered. "I can't believe I slept so long."

The wipers crossed the windshield, once, sweeping away a thin film of mist.

Every time they went to the beach, it rained.

"Hungry?" He tried again.

"I could use some coffee," Kay said.

The light changed. He watched streetlamps cameo her face, one after the other, opal light from glass globes on fluted iron stems. They were in a small dandified downtown. Trees were just coming into leaf in front of row houses. This place made its living from the kind of boutique history that could be sold to tourists, history so familiar and tangible it might be weighed out by the pound or folded up like yard goods. A sentimentalized Civil War. The only kinship it had to the broken mill towns of the

Monongahela Valley was that chance meeting of brick and sky.

"Looks like it's all shut up for the night," he said.

Kay stopped for another traffic signal. He considered his own reflection in the tinted window, eyes immersed in shadow, a receding hairline leaving his forehead to loom dramatically.

Gerard looked past himself to a man standing under a colonial portico, pillars blue with the glow from a 24-hour teller. Hand poised at the cash mouth, the man seemed to be a mannequin, advertising money as others did suits.

They turned left, following the arrow for the Maryland state highway east. The preserved area (Gerard thought it a good word, as though the past had been put by in heavy syrup) gave way to brightly lighted plazas, burger places. The highway divided.

"This looks more likely," he said encouragingly.

Kay slowed opposite a Denny's, but the parking lot was full and she speeded up. His stomach growled. He looked at her quickly, almost said that there wasn't much left to choose from, that the town was coming to an end and the highway ahead offered nothing, but he didn't. So often these days, she met his suggestions like orders too long accepted, now to be challenged.

It would be easy to say the change came with her administrative job at the med center, but Gerard was honest with himself. It had started before that. Perhaps hitting 40 (which he hadn't, not yet) had sharpened her focus. She spoke about the future like a broker charged with investing a limited capital.

Her level brows were drawn down. She was concentrating on the road but he wondered if other drivers, in the second's glance of traffic, saw only an angry woman.

Suddenly, she pulled into the left-hand lane to make a turn through the median. He bent forward, looking past her. One of those old-fashioned aluminum diners was anchored to a dim parking lot by an addition that, though it had to be more recent, appeared to sag away from the polished curves of the original.

The place seemed familiar, of course, a blast from the past, the first flagship of the McFood empires, "Eat at Joe's. " Then he recognized the Viking ship, spasmodic in orange neon. The international symbol for smorgasbord pointed its dragon prow toward the blank end wall of a motel just across the parking lot.

"Last food before interstate," he intoned as she pulled into the nearly empty lot. "There aren't even any truckers this ..."

"I'm tired, okay?"

Silenced, he opened the door and got out.

He was shocked at how cold it was. A thin, whining wind drove the mist into his face and he turned away from it, shrugging his collar up. It seemed like a long way to the entrance. A few hard drops of rain came down.

Inside, the place was warm and close as a kitchen. Steam tables sweltered. Gerard took off his windbreaker and hung it up, but Kay didn't take off her jacket; she leaned on the empty candy counter by the register as though waiting for a take-out.

A sign in front of the folding panel that shut off the addition said "Dining Room Closed."

"Great service," she muttered, shifting her weight to the other foot.

Everything about her was in a hurry, caught like a film still, motion implicit in the actor's stance. Her coarse dark hair, very short now, the gray evident, was lifted and frozen into place with gel. Her portfolio/ purse on its shoulder strap angled behind her body, thrust there by her elbow.

Gerard wished he could ease the stress from her body as gently as he'd shade a line into grace with a few strokes of his pencil.

Kay glared at the stocky waitress who, coffeepot in hand, stood laughing with a family. The little boy wore a "Rocky" T-shirt and the waitress fisted her hand, let him spar against it.

"Any time tonight."

The waitress must have heard. She came over, a meaningless bit of smile fixed in place, seated them in a booth and poured coffee without being asked.

"Cream?"

"Yes," Kay said abruptly.

Gerard reached across the table and pressed his spread fingers against her arm, twice, a private gesture. Count ten.

She slumped self-consciously in the seat, making a point of it, but her jaw was set with the pride of having pushed forward, driven into the dark and the rain that came steadily now against the windows.

The waitress came back with a metal cream pitcher and two menus under her arm. "Most folks want the smorgasbord, a' course." Her accent was decidedly southern. Almost falsely so.

"I'll take the smorgasbord," Gerard said.

"I will too." Kay answered his look, saying, "Must be the rain. I'm starved."

Gerard closed the menu. Faded gold lettering on the cover said "EVER-OPEN RESTAURANT – Never Closed – AT YOUR SERVICE."

He shut Kay's menu in her hand and touched the slogan.

"We were here before …"

"… on our honeymoon," she completed, with a weary little smile as if to say, of course I remember things, too.

"You were asleep when we pulled in that morning. I thought maybe you didn't remember."

"It was raining."

"It always rains."

"Ever-Open," she said, lingering on the words. "We said thank God for that, because nothing else was."

"We had to sit at the counter, it was that busy. And we drank so much coffee we had to stop twice down the road."

"We were poor, remember?" There was only a little edge to her teasing. "Stuffed ourselves at breakfast so we could skip lunch. Speaking of stuffing …"

She went first and he stayed in the booth to watch her purse. He stirred what looked like real cream into his coffee

Gerard remembered driving that night, over the mountains, the Front dropping into foothills, the rumpled land smoothing itself toward the coast. Sixteen years ago. A honeymoon on borrowed money five days between her graduation and the start of her first nursing job. Kay had slept while he drove, curled in the front seat of the Fury with her head on the center armrest. When he put his hand out to touch her, during the long hours with the AM radio very low, she'd lifted her body softly against his hand.

He watched her moving around the steam table. Now when he drove at night she stayed militantly awake, watching, she said, for deer. Her eyes were bright and alert as the eyes of animals on the berm, awake, awake, and he always remembered the Advent hymn although the accident had happened later, after Christmas.

Awake, awake, and somewhere behind the brightness of her eyes the fear. Waking as the car left the road, tires spinning, gravel slewing and then a brief bite of the blacktop before the car went finally off the road, nosing into a small frozen stream. And Kay, who had not screamed, unlocked her fingers from the dash and turned to him and stared without blinking. Her mouth open, she'd breathed the hard, short breaths of a laboring woman.

He said again that he'd not had too much to drink; he was just tired, his mind elsewhere. He never saw the deer until the buck's polished antlers had blazed in the headlights.

Gerard turned from late December chill, back to the warm evening on that first drive to the coast. Her sweet diffidence when she woke up. "Where are we? Okay," and then back to sleep, letting the long night scroll past unwatched. He saw her unlined forehead glow with highway lights, then fade back into shadow, faintly green from the dash indicators. He wanted to hold the vision – wanted, he realized, to fix it on paper.

"The ham looks dry," she said as she set her plate down, "but the roast beef is nice and pink."

He got up as she slid into the booth and went to circle the buffet.

Steam curled above trays of breaded, deep-fried chicken, and succotash, mashed potatoes, sauerkraut. Mom-food, Gerard thought as he filled his salad bowl. Pan rolls. Stuffing. Starch and fat without a second thought, just look at the butter (probably margarine) pooling around all the vegetables. He took chicken and roast beef and manicotti.

They ate without speaking. They ate as though there would not be another Ever-Open all the way to North Carolina. The waitress came several times, heavy-footed, to refill their cups.

"Why did I think I wanted that?" he said, pushing away the last of a piece of chocolate cake. A yawn took him.

Kay said, "Maybe we should have waited until morning."

He yawned again, thinking, you could have fit in another meeting or two, then berating himself for the unspoken cheap shot. People relied on Kay. "We'd have had the weekend travel," he said. "We beat it by leaving when we did."

Kay went to the rest room. He pushed the crumbs around on the plate and stared at her empty seat. Splits in the black vinyl were pulled together with duct tape.

He doodled with his finger on the tabletop. He'd never wanted to be anything but an artist. On the day she graduated, Kay had said she couldn't ever imagine being anything but a nurse. Maybe he just never learned to raise his expectations.

A painting of an American eagle clutching arrows and olive branches hung on the wall opposite the booth. There was a little piece of paper in the corner, $30, and he wondered who would buy such a stiff rendering. It reminded him of the Currier & Ives calendar from the insurance agent that always hung in his parents' kitchen. Everything so carefully delineated, steamboats motionless on rivers, skaters locked eternally in each other's arms, forgotten racehorses neck and neck at full stretch.

Gerard saw the little calico print of that kitchen wallpaper, a pattern from his childhood. His mother used to give him the roll-ends and he would weight the curling edges and draw on the back, horses usually. Even his childish attempts weren't as stiff as the striving animals in those Currier & Ives prints. He used to sign them Gerard, never Jerry. His father had called him Jerry when he came home after his shift, picking him up with strong arms that smelled of smoke and metal.

He watched Kay coming down the aisle between the counter and the booths until she caught him watching.

"That explains it," she said, patting the table with a possessive air of discovery, of holding a secret.

"Explains what?"

She tilted her head toward the rest of the all-but-empty diner, the two waitresses huddled with the cook.

"They're closing up. I heard them talking as I came by. They can't compete with the fast-food places."

Gerard realized he must have known that from the minute they came in. The candy counter, stripped but for a few rolls of antacid. The tightly controlled smiles. That strange remark by the old guy, sitting with his cronies, who told the counter waitress, "They won't put up with your mouth at the Holiday Inn." They'll learn to, she'd shot back.

"The Ever-Open closes its doors. A relic dies in a town where they'd put horse droppings in a museum," he said.

Kay laughed. "That's what I call worshipping the past."

But he was serious, at least partially. He disliked the smug, smiling, edited history in this town, these kinds of towns.

He thought of Homestead, Monessen, Irwin, Clairton, aging and dying with a raw dignity. Those names were names of strength, of the molten slag that used to light up the river and the sky all along the Mon and Ohio and Allegheny, machines that spoke in elemental hisses and roars and thumps and screams.

Sometimes, inside those blackened industrial shells he was depicting for the historical foundation, he saw faces flashed bright by steel in the pour. He felt an old urge to do paintings instead of illustrations, but the subject had changed.

Once he had wanted to paint wilderness untouched by the grime and shove of cities. Once there'd been no beauty in the mills.

Now he imagined faces, familiar faces of big-bellied men who had fallen from catwalks into wells of metal, all their raucous days flaring into a brief spike of alien organics in the steel. Plain sensible working people, men and women, their eyes a little wary from the knocks, but eager anyway. Looking ahead.

"That talk about preserving the works – it won't happen. We got more sense in the Valley. People'll take crowbars to the mills themselves before they get shut up in the past that way."

"What brought that on?" Kay asked, eyes widening at the unexpected fierceness.

"On my mind, I guess," he said, for lack of an explanation.

She sipped from her water glass. "I don't know how this place has hung on this long. Or why. But I'm kind of sorry it won't be here when we come back through."

The restaurant was quiet except for the clatter in the kitchen. The family had left. A hound-faced trucker came in, the seat of his jeans baggy from long sitting. He put his elbows on the counter. He looked like the men in Chiodo's Tavern, lost among the magpie artifacts of Homestead streets.

Gerard saw Kay looking toward the trucker and he wanted to reassure her, say, it's okay because there's a truck driver eating here, a rule of the road you pointed out the first time, but her eyes moved past in the politeness of not seeing.

The waitress steered toward them with the coffee pot and he put a hand over his cup.

"That be all for you folks?"

"I think so."

"You be careful driving, now." She walked away with the gait of someone who's broken down the sides of too many pairs of shoes.

"The last of the 24-hour diners," he said, watching.

"Well, this food went out in the '50s," reflected Kay. "Not a bean sprout or low-fat dressing in sight. We're talking antique."

It's not antique, he argued to himself, just common. Common as dirt, common as a kitchen in a neighbor's home where all the sooty frame houses were alike from street to street. Enduring, it would seem, but like that flickering neon ship, the commonplace had frozen into a symbol. Life went right on taking itself elsewhere. The ceaseless flow of semis that would have stopped here twenty years ago made the windows shudder as they rolled by. People in the booths could see the glass vibrate as they sat too long with their coffee, just for the warmth of it in their hands.

Gerard picked up the ticket, glanced at it. Coffee must be included. He left a big tip.

"You can have the check, if you're wanting," the waitress said as she rang it up. Printed at the top were "The EVER-OPEN," and a drawing of a fat Norseman in a horned helmet. "Some folks do, for a souvenir."

Gerard almost told her about stopping there on their honeymoon. In the pause, Kay looked at him and grinned, one side of her mouth curling higher than the other, and he knew she was thinking the same thing.

The woman shrugged and spiked the bill.

Now they noticed the small, hand-printed note on the door, and Gerard recalled the flutter of paper as they came in. "The EVER-OPEN Restaurant will close at 12 midnite. Going out of business. Thank you all for the good years."

Rain had faded back into mist. The breeze was welcome after the summery heat of the restaurant – bracing, Gerard decided, like sea air whipping over the Outer Banks that shifted but held against the tides.

They stood behind the car, Gerard on the driver's side, and he asked, "Want me to take it for a while?"

"Thanks," Kay said softly. "I'm beat." He heard keys jangle as they dropped to the bottom of her purse.

They got in and he started the engine. The steering wheel was alive under his hands.

Kay leaned gratefully back in her seat, head against the headrest. Her throat was long and slender, almost gaunt, tendons evident under the skin. And beautiful, like the texture of lines penciled at the outer corners of her eyes.

Gerard saw a break in the traffic, swung out and headed east.

EDGES

~

THEY SAID THAT, DOWN INSIDE the concrete wall of the dam, there was a crack.

Not dangerous, at this point, but maybe after more years and spring floods and the long pressure of water, then it would be dangerous. So the Army Corps of Engineers had opened the gates and spilled the lake water down the river, past the mill town where they lived.

She was with him, sitting quietly in the passenger seat, her cheek pressed against the window. She had asked to come along. He had wanted to come here by himself, to see that land that had been under water so long. Since his mother's time was the way he thought of it–his mother had been a young woman living on a farm in this river valley when the dam took the land.

He parked the car by the boat ramp and they walked down the sloping concrete until it ended, impossibly far from the thread of water in the old river channel. Then they walked down the bottom of the lake.

This had been a deep valley, a real cut through the hills. The winter wind was stronger here, funneled between the steep slopes of the ridges, cold and sharp. It honed the edges of broken glass that stuck up out of the mud, shards of beer bottles thrown out of boats. It whipped her long hair so that she walked in a blonde foam. She pushed her hands back along the curve of her skull and captured the tossing hair, twisted it and stuffed it back down inside the collar of her jacket. In a minute it was out again. She smiled tentatively, her eyes narrowed against the wind and the wild lashing hair.

The mud sucked at their boots. There was less glass as they walked deeper into the emptied lake. The trash was up high, like on a shelving beach when the tide goes out. The empty shells and debris were always piled in rows along the beach, while out on the flats were slippery stones, colonies of seaweed and the air holes of creatures buried since the last tide.

The lake bottom was barren and useless. There were stumps that had been trees, and raw channels cut in the mud by the brash new streams that ignored the paths of the ones which once ran to a river.

Edges were the productive places, tidal zones, marshes, the cattail places and the muddy banks of streams where crawfish are hunted by otters and raccoons. He had begun trapping again, after the mill closed, something he hadn't done since he was a kid. Fur prices were better, now, but the animals were fewer. There weren't as many swamps and bogs, the places that were half water and half land and thick with life. They were either drowned or drained, like this.

A single gull flew overhead; she pulled at his sleeve and followed its path with her finger. It screamed once, as though her finger had been a weapon, as though a bullet had come from it and struck the gull and it was dying. It wheeled left and went out over the thread of water.

"I didn't know there were gulls here," she shouted above the wind.

"Sometimes, around big lakes."

She nodded.

He could no longer see their car. They had walked a long way.

"It makes me think of the beach," she said.

"Yeah."

She had never been to the ocean until he took her to a beach resort for their honeymoon. It had been crowded with people, thick with the smell of suntan oil and spilled soda, noisy with a hundred radios playing. He thought the gull was not much of a connection between that strip of rumpled sand, shadowed by hotel towers, and this bare place scoured by the wind.

He bent down and worked something free of the mud. The shape of it had caught his eye. He took it to a shallow pool and swished it back and forth, until the water was muddy and the object half clean. It was a teacup, white with a familiar pattern of pink roses around the rim. He turned it over and read the manufacturer – one that had gone out of business thirty years ago, in their own town.

"It's not even cracked," she said, putting her hand out to touch its smooth curve.

"Yeah, well." He scrubbed at a spot of dirt with his thumb. His hands were chilled from the water. He put the cup in the big front pocket of his sweatshirt.

They walked over a rise in the lake bottom, once some farmer's hillside field too steep for plowing, and then the bass fisherman's structure, a ragged line on a depth finder. And now a muddy slope.

A man was working down on the next flat, close to a broad fan of concrete that had been the swimming area. He ranged back and forth across the bottom, like a bird dog, his head bent and his arms extended to hold a metal detector above the mud.

"He's not gonna get anything but cold," he said.

She turned her face toward him and then away as the wind struck it.

"Why?" she asked, her voice fading as she turned.

"This lake's filling up with mud. Anything dropped there last summer would be three feet deep by now."

"He's got a shovel," she pointed out.

The man stopped, swung his detector back and forth slowly, then hiked it under his arm and began to scrape at the mud with the shovel.

"He's a persistent somebody," he said, watching the man work through the mud, layer at a time. "You'd think he was after Blackbeard's treasure."

The man knelt, picked something up and put it in his pocket.

"Pieces of eight, arrrr, matey," he mocked.

They turned back from the rise and began to follow a band of rocky ground along the slope and down toward the river bed.

Why should I laugh at the poor guy, he asked himself. I've got about as much chance of finding another job as he does of digging up buried treasure.

The cold wind slicing over the open ground made his ears ache and his nose drip. He sniffed twice and then rubbed his sleeve across the numb end of his nose.

Mud. We're all stuck in mud. Out of work and can't leave because half the town's out of work and so who would buy the house or any of a hundred others? He wondered if the man with the metal detector was a mill hand, too, and decided that probably he was. That was why he was looking for coins or jewelry. Something to bring in a little cash. Something to do on a Tuesday morning when Tuesdays past had been occupied with work.

The rocky path disappeared and they were back in mud. This part of the lake had only recently emptied. The mud was thick and brown, oozing up around the soles of their boots. The river channel was 200 yards away, the water shimmering and clean, reflecting the gray sky and breaking its plain face up into facets of light and dark, waves and patterns.

He could no longer hear the sucking sound of the mud as it released her boots. She had stopped.

He turned around.

"I don't think we can get down to the water," she said, her voice pitched to carry over the howl of the wind.

"It's not too bad."

"It looks awful wet."

He went back to walking, picking out the dry spots as he veered across the flat toward the water. The mud got deeper, began to have that surface shimmer of quicksand, smooth and appearing deceptively solid.

He was stopped halfway to the water. The last step took had taken him down calf-deep in the slop and he had only barely pulled his boot free. Liquid mud trickled down his leg as he stood staring at the old river, moving along toward the dam as though that failing concrete wall wasn't there, never had been there.

He stuck his hands in the front pocket and felt the teacup. It wasn't right, that a piece of white china should have stayed unbroken all those years. He wanted to take it and throw it down against a stone, smash it, so that the world would be in balance again. It was the little things that made the world spin crooked, it was the tiny horned devils of improbability. He fingered the delicate handle and the smooth joint where it met the bowl.

She was no longer with him. He knew that she had gone back. He stared at the unapproachable river until the glow of the overcast sky on water made his burning eyes close involuntarily.

He put his head down and began to walk back to the car. She was there already, probably, had the heater doing and her boots off, warming her feet.

He slogged out of the deep stuff, across the stony ground, and back onto firm mud as the bottom rose toward the lake edge and the road.

When he looked up to get his bearings, he saw her walking out of a cove, carrying something white.

What could she have found? It looked the size of a quart Clorox jug, the kind that people used for floats. She held it tucked in the crook of her arm, the way you carry a cat, or a baby.

He angled back so their paths would cross.

Now he could see the thing was pointed. It was smooth and pointed, like a massive spear head made out of quartz. He kept his eye on it. The shape and color made him wonder, made him walk faster toward her, and she was walking faster now and no longer moving aimlessly across the barren plain.

She lifted the thing she had found. It was a gull wing, he could recognize it at last, the white feathers edged with yellowish-brown mud. He wondered how it had come there.

Maybe a fox had killed the bird. Foxes were opportunists. They would follow the edge of the water, picking up a living from frogs or carrion, or a gull that waited too long to lift from its own meal on a stranded fish.

She lifted the severed wing high in the air and spread the feathers. The long primaries portioned out wedges of the gray sky. He smiled, just a little, because his lips were chapped by the wind and split as he smiled.

He put his arm around her as they walked back to the car. She was cold and shivered as he embraced her. She kept the gull wing, holding it up in front of them like a trophy, or the flame of a torch that sometimes stands stiffly as a flag in the wind.

ACT OF GRACE

~

SOMEONE BROUGHT A BOX OF DOUGHNUTS to the office this morning. The rich compound of fat and sugar drifted over cubicle walls, disseminating like the jasmine drench of that commercial air freshener with which donut-smell is, for me, forever entwined – deep in that limbic forest where no one ever plans to go but is somehow directed.

I went to the break table and opened the box. Thirteen donuts, unevenly distributed in their rows. I could identify each one without tasting, recognized the thin red smear of jelly filling (put in plenty of jelly if they ask for a mixture, Mr. Schenck always said) and recalled its cheap metallic aftertaste.

I saw Naomi's hands, nail-bitten, gloved in honey glaze.

~

Naomi was the night finisher at the donut shop where I worked in my sophomore year. I had counter duty on the third shift, 11 p.m. to 7 a.m., which left me time to walk home, shower and catch the bus to make my early class nearly all the time. Naomi worked an odd schedule, 5 p.m. til 1 a.m. She refilled the emptied racks and stacked tray after tray of doughnuts on carts in the back room, so that we would have enough for the rush after the bars closed and for the mill hands who brought steel Thermoses to be filled with coffee in the morning.

In the quiet hour around midnight, the only sounds in the place were the bubble of the fruit punch cooler and the bang and slam of Naomi lifting galvanized bins of toasted coconut and cinnamon-sugar onto the finishing bench.

Occasionally she would come out front and serve when we were busy, or if one of us waitresses was on break, but she didn't like it. Naomi wore a heavy steel-and-leather brace on her left leg, withered knee to ankle. We imagined childhood polio, her parents somehow having kept her from immunization. She moved deftly enough and her handicap didn't seem to be the reason for her reticence.

Most times, she was a face at the tray window. "Chocolate-iced cake," we'd yell, or "More cream-filled," and she would slide a neat paper-lined tray through the opening. She would always lean down to make sure someone was there, and for that moment her face was framed and backlit by the harsh fluorescents of the finishing room: perfectly heart-shaped like the makeover sketches in *Glamour*, with her long hair pulled back and neatly capped by a hairnet one shade too dark.

∾

Naomi was beautiful, actually. She wasn't glamorous, with her crippled leg and her hairnet, and her apron smeared with sweet offal. But she had an intrusive kind of beauty, eyes that seemed a bit wild, too much white showing, set far apart like Jackie Kennedy's under a broad forehead. Her hair was glossy and very thick – the kind of brown that makes you reject "auburn" and think instead of the names they give to horses, chestnut or roan or sorrel. She wore it loose except at work, when she plaited it into a single braid that swung heavily across her back.

I told her once that she should have it cut, and she asked me why. I couldn't tell her the truth, that shorter hair would make her seem less primitive, less perturbing; instead, I made up something about the spring look.

Her beauty lay on bones that might have fit the Neolithic, but ethereal too, like the severe angels of medieval manuscripts borne on a pair of upraised wings while a second pair crosses in front of their bodies, shielding their virtue.

Her body, like her face, was excessive, the body not of those masculine angels but the more recent and voluptuously female type of Christmas angel, with flowing draperies outlining breasts and generous hips. She was shorter than me by several inches but we wore the same size. She gave an impression of over-ripeness, her uniform taut across her breasts but too big around her waist, material pleating under the strings of her apron.

I wrote a paper – "Love Calls Us to the Things of This World: Images of Angels." The title came from a poem I came across at the library. My thesis was that popular imagination had used angels to reintroduce the female to an aggressively male theology. The Michaels and Uriels and Gabriels of the Old Testament, warriors and heralds, had become neuters and then buxom females with streaming blonde hair. I got a B – not enough documentation, though the professor liked my ideas.

I'm a blonde, myself, but my hair was never what you'd call luxuriant. In college I began wearing it long, though every time I brushed it I could hear my mother say, "Roberta, LENGTH takes out ALL the BODY." She had owned a beauty salon when I was in grade school. I used to sit in the row of plastic-covered chairs beside women whose heads were elaborately ranked with curlers, letting the hot wind from the dryers ruffle my hair razored close as a boy's.

Men would flirt with Naomi when she was out front. They were attracted by the hair and the startled eyes and the breasts. Then, as she walked away, returning to the kitchen heat that flushed her cheeks, they saw the withered leg in its metal casing.

The men became either silent or loud, aggressive. The loud ones hit on whoever was available. Me, or fat Patsy, who appreciated the deflected lust.

∽

I thought a lot about symbols back then. Archetypes. I was majoring in psychology, because I thought you could be taught to understand people and why they did the things they did. Later I changed to social work, where you only have to deal with the consequences.

That spring, my early class was political science – "American Political Parties in the 20th Century." Pretty much everyone knew the course was cake, easy credits. Most of the class was made up of football players.

The instructor had been married once, for a short and childless time, to another faculty member. Now she was holding back middle age with Lady Clairol and defiance. She never sat at the desk or used the podium, but walked restlessly around the tables arranged in a horseshoe, leaning over male students to point out interesting parts of the text. One of the guys, my friend and sometime drinking companion, would ask her questions, then flash a grin my way as she bent helplessly close to him.

I remember that she wore miniskirts long after they were "out." That, and the luster of heavy agate beads against her leathery tan. She went to the Bahamas every spring break, and there were pretty solid rumors that she paid the fare for a male companion, sometimes one of those same football players.

Though I considered using her as a case study, "Female A," for my sexuality class, I didn't. Even in a college of that size, things get around.

～

Naomi had plenty of boyfriends, sometimes the very ones who'd gone silent as she backed through the door with a load of empty trays, shouldering it open then swinging her stiff leg through the closing gap.

She had no artifice. She never wore makeup, though ChapStick and hand lotion were acceptable in winter. Gerry who worked in the kitchen at The Quail's Nest said he heard she was born Old Order Amish, but that her family had been shunned. I could imagine her hair shadowed by one of those black bonnets, face and body concealed, a carnal nun with three or four apple-cheeked children already at 20. I could imagine that easily, but I didn't believe what Gerry said. Truth just slipped through those soft hands of his, whitened by dishwater.

Men came to the back door of the donut shop like bums hoping for a bleary sack of day-olds. In the summer when Naomi took her dinner break she would sit on the back stoop with them, I think to avoid the smell of stale cigarettes from the ashtrays. I didn't smoke, but at that time it didn't bother me as it does now.

The back stoop wasn't exactly a picnic area. When the wind was out of the south there was the waft of trash from the dumpster around the corner of the building. The view across the alley was directly into the stage door of The Vixxen Club.

The backs of the buildings that fronted on High looked as though they'd never been finished, just cheaply closed in and left to darken with coal smoke and rain. They all looked alike, except that in summer the stage door was often open at the Vixxen, (a converted furniture store) and women moved past the opening like slides in one of those projectors before the Carousel was invented – naked or costumed, or in the camouflage of street clothing.

~

Now this is the strange thing. Of all the jobs I've held, in college and after college, I remember the donut shop the best. I remember it intimately, with every sense, the way men say they recall a particular perfume blended with the skin-scent of a former lover.

The odor of hot fat was everywhere. It clung to hair and clothes. Grease popped from the frying tanks and was pulled into the fans, coating them so that dust quickly wooled the metal cages.

And though the smells were bakery smells, vanilla and cinnamon and chocolate, the sounds were closer to those of the nearby factories. The arrival of Casimir, the night baker, brought a thumping chorus of the Hobart mixer and the rolling machine, and the liquid "kachunk" of the cruller machine dropping twisted dough into the fryer. The crullers looked like carnival pinwheels caught in the act of unfurling, their spirals fat and unformed as the wings of emerging moths.

I remember the way my hands were always sticky with sugar and spilled coffee, and how the counter rags would turn sour despite the constant wiping of sweet crumbs. White shoes were stiffened by dabs of frosting and fresh glaze.

The floors were covered with terrazzo tile. The baker's duties included scraping up the sticky crust with a kind of long-handled putty knife and then mopping.

We closed the place twice a year to "redd up proper," as Mrs. Schenck always said. July and December. That year, a windy snowstorm hit on the night of the winter cleaning.

I had to climb on the tables to wipe down the metal frames around the windows – Naomi couldn't step up, Patsy was too clumsy, and the men wouldn't do it. I remember leaning against the glass and holding tight to the frames, dizzied by swirling snow, the unpredictable blasts against the windows. It seemed that I could fall through into that formlessness and be lost.

This is something: We ground the coffee beans fresh for each pot, just like the chain shops. I recall very clearly grinding several portions of coffee, and as the steel blades whirled the beans into powder, I tried to imagine being 25, 35, 40. I would be a psychologist at 25, director of a treatment center when I was 30. The buildings would all be one story and spread across landscaped acres, like a college campus. After that, nothing. Forty was a blur.

I didn't imagine Lewis, though I was sure I'd get married sometime. I didn't imagine him slipping so easily into violence, the flat of his hand and then the clench of it. I couldn't imagine following my mother into early divorce, or becoming for a time so familiar with the scent of spilled beer and abandoned cigarettes that it sickens me today.

∾

My social circle, which was pretty much limited to the guys from school, expanded when Naomi and I became friends in those two slow hours each night. She started taking me with her on Saturday jaunts to bars outside town – the dance club at Crystal Lake, roadhouses where construction workers drank, or fraudulent chalets in the mountains that served beer in steins and hot dogs they called "wurst."

Naomi seldom had dates with the men who came to see her, though she often met up with one of them at a bar or club.

We were independent women. We bought our own drinks, unless we felt like accepting them from men who leaned across the bar, grinning, to see our faces when the sloe gin fizzes arrived. I guess they thought that, being women, we'd like them. Pink and sweet.

Naomi was fearless. She would drive anywhere, in any weather, and always too fast. The gas tank was seldom more than quarter-full. Her car was a Dodge Dart as anonymous as any on the streets. It was a faded dark green with a mint green interior. She called it the Frog Prince. In the winter, she said, she had to open the hood and kiss the carburetor to make it start.

She loved to dance. A textbook might have labeled it denial. She wore the long skirts briefly popular at the time, and danced on crowded floors where her handicap didn't matter.

One time at the Powder-Keg there was a live band, a good one. They'd made a record but it had not sold well (a promotion rip-off, according to Grey who was the lead singer) so they were back on the local circuit. The bassist was new, from another failed group. He was meltingly beautiful, a boy-child, a curly-headed Pan.

Naomi had had several of the austere gin-and-tonics she drank as though punishing herself for the intoxication. She was dancing with a lanky mechanic who was the newest of her conquests when the band closed a dance tune by spinning directly into one of its own riff-heavy anthems.

Her partner must have said something, because he headed for the rest-rooms. Naomi kept dancing. I saw my partner already nearing the bar, but the floor had cleared rapidly and only the two of us remained.

I was embarrassed for her, and so I stayed, dancing as the song went on and on. The lead singer shrieked, trying for Zeppelin heights but failing. The cords in the bassist's slender wrist were tight as he worked to fret the heavy strings of his instrument. I was afraid to look into his eyes. I felt superfluous, but unable to walk off the floor.

Naomi danced. Her swaying movements, as she rocked onto her crippled leg, were hypnotic as a shaman's limping sacrament.

When the song ended, the bassist had leaped from the stage and whirled her around and around.

∽

I don't believe that Naomi understood, any more than the rest of us, why so many men were attracted to her. She was beautiful, as I've said, but that is seldom enough. And Naomi was quiet, a shyness deep in her bones that emerged, not in blushes and stammers, but in silence. When she spoke her voice was too thin for her body.

Gerry said it was a fetish. Her leg, the brace. I told him he was wrong.

The women from the Vixxen understood fetishes. They chose outfits of leather or nurse white to titillate the men who required specifics for their pleasure. The strippers, when they came in after work, were rather plain, even childlike, playing with the sugar servers and giggling. They, too, required that plumage to carry off the conceit.

One of them had left a catalog in the restroom, where the jasmine air freshener squirted cloying aerosols around the clock. It was from a place that sold erotic clothing. I found it lying on the floor beside the commode.

I showed the catalog to Patsy, and we had some fun trying to figure out exactly how you'd walk in thigh-high boots with six-inch heels.

The boots and shoes ran all the way to size 13. There were false bodies in the catalog, breasts and rounded stomachs molded in plastic for men to strap across their flatness.

The catalog lay on the table in the break room for three days, among the copies of "Motor Trend" and "Cosmo." Mr. Schenck took it away and posted a memo about sexual materials in the workplace.

The items in that catalog were so bizarre – chains, black hoods that sealed off eyes and mouth, rubber suits, whips – that I couldn't believe men with such desires might be attracted by Naomi's limp or the industrial brace that enclosed that thin white limb.

Limb seemed a peculiarly appropriate word – a branch, an almost flesh-less extension that bore the weighty fruit of her foot in its black shoe.

~

Naomi especially liked making the "fancies" that were cradled in crisp paper in the display case. There were napoleons, layers of pastry and cream decorated with lattices of chocolate. And danishes, brushed with a shimmering glaze that seemed always at the verge of crystallization.

Donut cakes were popular, though I never understood why. Thick lumps of dough were cut in the vague shape of cartoon characters and fried. Naomi finger-painted them with frosting, a background color, then transformed them into Mickey Mouse or Spiderman with birdlike squirts from a pastry bag.

Naomi said she wished she could see the children's faces when her cakes arrived.

She never talked about her family, but Patsy told me (her sister was

with the State Health) that Naomi had an older sister who was immense-
ly fat and severely retarded. That's why Naomi didn't come to work until
5, when her father got home from his job. Someone had to stay with the
sister every minute. I pictured the sister as a smooth-faced and bloated
Naomi, blissful in her flesh as an idol.

Naomi's father worked at the water treatment plant, and preached
Sunday morning and evening at a storefront Pentecostal chapel. I saw
him once. He was a plain man in a green uniform, his jaw white with
tension, and you would have said there was nothing in common between
father and daughter but the sense that he, too, was obscurely crippled.

I remember that Naomi would sometimes have whispered conversa-
tions on the telephone. Her head would be tucked down against the wall
as she talked, holding all the words confessional between her mouth and
the receiver.

Once the women at the Vixxen ordered a donut cake for the club
manager's birthday. They brought in a cartoon of the Venus de Milo,
ripped out of some skin mag, the marble breasts adorned with oversized
pink nipples and the statue's cool expression altered to lasciviousness.
Whatever else had been in the picture had been ripped away.

Naomi asked me why the woman had no arms and I explained.

She did a creditable job of modeling white-on-white, using cream-col-
ored frosting to delineate fabric and figure. She mixed the pink frosting
and matched the picture.

Casimir came in when she was almost done.

"You made a mistake," he said.

She backed away, holding the twisted pastry bag high. "Where?"

He dragged his finger across one breast and lifted away the frosting
nipple. "She's only got one tit."

He stuck the tip of his finger in his mouth and sucked vigorously,
drawing his thin sallow face fleshless as a skull.

I laughed, and he sucked harder, moaning.

"M-mm-mother's milk," I said, half-choking.

"Ooohh, baby," he said, and strolled out of the finishing room.

Naomi never looked at me. She stepped forward and applied a new
nipple, first the aureole and then a dab atop that. Fully erect.

~

It was a Saturday evening, June or July, hot. And Naomi was late picking me up, which was unusual.

I heard the Frog Prince out front and pulled on my dress, feeling the polyester stick to me everywhere immediately.

Most times she would honk for me to come down, but that evening I heard the car door slam, then the side door of the house, then the step and clunk of Naomi climbing the stairs. She let herself in and flopped into the single chair.

"What gives?" I flexed my shoulders to lift the fabric away from my back.

"I wondered" – and she held her hand against her chest in mock exhaustion – "if you'd let me borrow that black dress. The one with the roses on it."

"Sure." I pulled the dress off its hanger and threw it across the daybed.

"Can I try it on?"

I nodded tersely, put out at the delay. "I need an aspirin."

"It's the heat," she said, but didn't make a move toward the dress.

I went into the bathroom.

The childproof cap wouldn't budge. I pried, trying not to break a fingernail. The polish chipped anyway. Finally the cap popped off and arced behind the water-heater.

The hell with it. I shook three tablets into my sweaty hand and swallowed them without water. Medicine was medicine, as Mom used to say.

"I have to go see the lawyer," Naomi said, her voice muffled .

Maybe she got a traffic ticket, the way she drove.

Sun slanted through the little window under the gable and pooled in the tub. I lifted my hair off my neck, twisted it up and held it against my head. No better. I put the bottle back on the shelf without the cap.

Maybe – and this came instantly, a truth terrible as the place where a dream begins again – maybe something had happened with her sister.

"What's this lawyer stuff?" I asked, casually enough, as I came out of the bathroom.

Naomi stood in the center of the room, nude. Her skirt and cotton blouse, slip and panties were on the floor at her feet. The dress was where I had left it. My honest gaze became slippery, slid away from her, focused on that black crumpled shape like her shadow thrown across the bed.

But because she was so still, I looked.

Her shoulders were wider than I'd realized, balancing the breadth of her hips. The shortness of her waist was not a flaw but a higher perfection – an archetype, all space devoted to breasts and belly and thighs.

The light came around her, tangled with the shadows of plants hanging in the windows. She was not tanned. There was no emphasis on her body but the dark wedge of her mons pointing to the cage around her withered leg.

Naomi lifted her arms and held them straight out to her sides, palms up; she stood there, poised like someone being fitted for clothing or otherwise measured.

I heard the brittle music of a childhood jewelry box, a gift from my father. The lid lifted, a pink ballerina (eyes painted shut) sprang up and began turning and turning in front of a shard of mirror. Slowing until at last she was motionless, arms out, facing her image and my own.

I remember lifting the hair off the back of my neck again. I was ready to cry with the heat, and the way my hair had gone limp, and how the smell of donuts was tattooed into my skin.

Naomi waited.

My heart said, "Angel, angel," and was afraid.

PAS DE DEUX

~

"HOLD STILL!" SHE SHOUTED as the cane lashed toward her. Jane caught a bunch of leaves, working her fingers past sopping roses and the wicked thorns.

She spread her other hand across Merrill's head. Thorns curved stubbornly into his wet hair and clutched at his shoulder. Rain gusted into her face, driven by the wind that had torn the rambler from its arch, whipping the cane into his path as they ran for shelter. Lightning flared, a shuddering thunder-roll. They jumped. He was free, but they both stood for a surprised moment, staring at the blonde hair skeined on the thorns.

They sprinted for the back door. Slippery flagstones. Black, she thought, like black glass on old storefronts. Rain runneling off the eaves. Through the sheaf of water, the pouring, pounding, down the back of the neck, cold, stinging like stones.

The door slammed and they were in a dim, airless, muffled space.

Merrill hit the top button of the old-fashioned light switch. A fluorescent ring glowed and flared greenish-white, darkening the windows.

"Damn that Queen Elizabeth," he said. "I should have taken a blowtorch to its roots."

"'Feed me,'" she quoted, in her deepest man-eating basso.

"Yeah," he said, standing there, breathing.

The lightning crack-boomed again, farther away, or maybe just distanced by the shelter of the slumping little back entry, an add-on filled with old clothes, a chest freezer, bushel baskets and folded bags.

Merrill peeled his soaked shirt away from one arm and down the other. His body was white and puckered cold from the storm. A raw scratch came over his shoulder, through the freckles and mottled damage from long-ago sun, and diagonally across his collarbone, weeping blood at individual points like the pricks of a needle.

Jane kicked off her sneakers, skinned out of her top, then her bra.

Merrill contemplated.

She took the two steps across that space, water squelching under the soles of her feet. She thrust her arms between his arms and body, his one hand on his hip still clutching the wet shirt. Jane leaned back to look in his face, then pulled him to her and rubbed her breasts back and forth on his cold chest. The shirt hit the linoleum like a mop.

He laughed as though being tickled, and Jane caught his laughter. Merrill rubbed his furry belly against her, damp and cool but warming, and howled with his head thrown back, setting them off again.

A crack like an axe through wood, incandescent sky, immediate thunder, and the lights slammed off. Blazed up. Off, on, off.

Jane's laughter went on a moment longer than his, very loud in the house where, although there had been no particular noise a moment before, the silence was sudden and physical.

They waited for the lights to come back, but this blackout was final. Rain drummed in a gust.

Jane pulled away from Merrill's loosely locked arms.

"Flashlights?"

"I wouldn't count on batteries," he said. "But there's candles and a kerosene lamp. Here."

He threw her an old flannel shirt from the peg near the door. Its arms spun out as it flew, and it collapsed softly in her hands. He took another and put it on.

Jane buttoned it partway, like a pajama top, the long tails hanging to her thighs as she dropped her jeans. She rolled back the sleeves. In the storm light, the pattern was gray over black.

He opened the kitchen door. It dragged on the threshold, a dry-rot sound that seemed impossible in the monsoon beating against the walls. Merrill let her go through first.

There was even less light here, only a small window over the sink shaded by a yard crowded with old trees. It was impossible to see any-thing but heavy branches, clots of dark leaves; still, the outside had more light. She oriented herself by the white boxes of stove, refrigerator, the roll-out dishwasher.

"I think the candles are in the drawer by the sink," Merrill said, close behind, or so it seemed, but he was still in the doorway and she was already moving.

She opened a drawer. Silverware. In the one below, knives.

"The other side," he said, walking behind her, and she turned, they bumped, she apologized, as though he might have been his father, tot-tering around the kitchen with buttons undone, peering into familiar cabinets for something he couldn't put a name to. She pulled open a drawer.

"Ta-daah." Merrill held up a pair of tapers, of some indeterminate color.

She looked back down at the drawer balanced on her grasp. Utensils. A mass of metal like foundry scraps. Handles and knobs. A small cage – she turned it over, an eggbeater, stained dark, as though it were made of wood, not metal. These were old implements used by his parents, maybe grandparents.

"I'll get candle holders," he said. "The matches are over the stove."

She had seen the tin dispenser, spotted with grease, the sides cut out for lighting wooden kitchen matches on the side of the box. Jane struck a match; it fizzed into flame. Merrill held out a candle stuck in a short bottle. She touched the flame to the long wick. It curled under, black-ened, and the light widened to fill the room.

"You lose the power often?" she asked, as she lit the second candle. It tilted in the jam jar.

"Not often. But when we do, it can stay out for a while. The road floods and they can't get in from the town side," Merrill said. For a mo-ment his eyes looked black, impenetrable, then he tilted his head and the light caught the green. She felt the whump in her stomach.

"That storm came up awfully fast," she said, bending sideways over the sink as she stripped water from her long hair, the droplets falling like honey in that light. "If it hadn't been for the lightning, I might have pulled you down and rolled you over under the trees for a quick one."

"Screwing in wet grass sounds better than it is," he said, his voice flat as though recording some observation.

She had only half-meant it, an enticement.

Merrill lifted the globe from the kerosene lamp, a hurricane lamp is what she would have called it. The flame spread along the cotton wick, smoky and twisting high. He turned the knob until the wick was low and the flame broadened and bloomed into even light.

~

They went inward, to the living room, away from the darkening sky and the renewed heavy rain, leaving one candle on the drain board. It dripped onto the porcelain as it tilted in the mouth of the jar. She held the other candle.

Though he was carrying the lamp, Merrill automatically reached past the doorframe and pressed the button for the lights. He smiled, pushing the lower button, then the top again, back and forth, a little dance of playfulness.

The living room was more like a storeroom: a faded Colonial suite from the previous generations, a listing recliner, a hundred-year-old wooden rocker, red leather ottoman, the soft couch that Merrill added when he inherited the home place. The sofa was directly in front of the fireplace, and Jane turned sideways to avoid its cold dark gape. She faced Merrill, leaning back against the arm of the couch as she finger-combed her wet hair back and twisted it at the nape of her neck.

It had been humid earlier, as they walked to the woods, the air heavy with the storm. Now a chill shivered across her. Jane crossed her arms on her chest. The fireplace breathed dampness. Maybe they could start a fire. But no, it wasn't cold, it was just her. Wet hair, wet feet, bare legs.

Merrill sat, looking straight ahead, sunk into another silence.

Jane shifted, turning on her center to lie against him. He put an arm around her shoulders and she nestled into the comfortable pit of his body.

His breath eased in and out. She matched hers to his, then felt them drift out of synch.

Merrill moved, then lifted himself away, his hip losing contact with hers, the embrace of his arm suddenly friendly rather than loving. Her side was damp where the wet had crept through from his cutoffs.

"I think a tree went down on the lines," he said.

"Umm?"

"The way the lights went out and came back. That's something hitting and lifting, a tree, or a pole breaking. The lights are down across the lake, so it had to be past Acklin Crossing. Or it could be on Old Lantzville Road."

She didn't know where he meant. She knew what Lantzville was, a cluster of strip malls surrounded by development, but couldn't picture these places as he did, Lantzville, Acklin Crossing. He was the native, at the center of a familiar world. He had it all pulled around him like a quilt.

Jane used to know names and places. She had been at ease in the place she'd grown up. Then she'd gone away to school, worked, moved, married. After the divorce, she had come to this boomtown, pulled by a new job. The first time the moon rose, she'd cried because it had surprised her in the window above her bed, like in the window of her girlhood room.

"You can tell the road's flooded," he said. "Hear the roar over the outlet?"

She realized that steady pulse of sound no longer came from the rain. It was running water, a waterfall spilling over the flat bridge between the two lakes, the dam and outlet that ran from one to the other. She imagined the water sweeping over the top of the dam, over the bridge, cutting off the one-lane road where people, meeting in their cars, pulled aside onto worn crescents of dirt to let the other by.

Merrill's grandfather had built this house, adding wings onto a settler cabin and facing the whole thing with stone. Merrill's father, a farmer as well, had passed along to him the knowledge of forest sounds, the times when wildflowers bloomed or hay should be cut. Merrill was deep in this place, his family and friends dotted across a map that was a raised relief of emotion and event.

All her new friends were rootless, except for Merrill, all of them buccaneering in the glass towers that rose along the parkway, apart from the old downtown and its Depression-era storefronts. They were doing well, as people do when they are smart and quick and they win jobs in new places far from home.

Maybe it was fear that kept Merrill in this familiar place. Or maybe, she admitted, it was a kind of wisdom.

Jane felt her freedom catch a cold wind and rise, not quite out of control.

She reached over and touched his arm. He turned and the opening of his shirt showed the brier scratch. She followed the mark with the tip of her finger, down, across the curve of collarbone. Had it ever been broken, like hers, one side in a fall from a tree one summer, the other from a football tumble the next? The scratch plunged straight from his shoulder, like an anchor rope into the depths of his chest hair.

"It's a bad scratch," she said, finally.

"That rosebush has been there forever. The canes get so thick, and the thorns. It's out of control," he said.

She weighed the reluctance in his voice. Was it because of its age and beauty that he wouldn't prune the rose, or the family history of its planting and care, or fear of its massive stems and curving thorns?

"You could get a landscaping service," she suggested.

"Have the summer youth workers take a machete to it, more likely."

She remembered the raw road-edges on the drive over, the uneven pale stubble of cut brush and weeds. The workers in their orange mesh vests, their lean bodies that should be strong but looked like those of cave creatures, soft, white, incapable of the cleared miles expected of them.

∼

She stood at the sink, drinking the cold water, tasting stone. It came from a spring, no chlorine.

The dog's double bowl was empty. She ran her glass full, twice, pouring it into the water bowl. Where was Skinner? He was a big, rough dog, part Newfoundland, with a lug head and a habit of sitting his entire dead weight on your foot. Probably in the barn, getting his coarse fur full of hay.

The appliances seemed to swell, the thin candlelight making them fluoresce like white flowers in the night garden. They were full of a restrained presence. Everything seemed to wait for the refrigerator to groan into its cycle, for the water heater to make the pipes sing. The digital clock on the stove showed the same three numbers. The old electric clock over the sink that usually chirred like an insect was still, the hands pointing.

"Do you want anything?" she called.

"No. I'm fine."

Merrill was dramatically set in shadow, lit like a movie hero with lamplight from one side, the soft fill of the candle from the other, the planes of his face honed by the invisible. The bump midway down the bridge of his nose was highlighted. His hair coiled, Viking ringlets, released from its usual control by the rain.

Jane bent towards him, her brown hair flaring red where it fell in front of her eyes, across his arm. He touched the end of her hair, then stroked it down from the top of her head, slowly. A momentary heat. She leaned her head toward his touch. She waited, but Merrill was looking somewhere just past her, like a sleepwalker. Her mouth opened toward his, her fingers curled to follow the curve of his ear, but she paused. She must have trembled or made some movement, because Merrill looked up at her and she turned away, feeling the flush of confusion in her face.

Jane stepped back, sat in the recliner, tucked her legs under her buttocks. The chair tilted, slightly off-balance.

∾

Everything went on at a distance. The storms prowled on the horizon, lightning shimmering from cloud to cloud. The frogs chorused. Down in the woods, the thrush began to sing. He called the bell-bird, but to her the tone was electronic and discordant.

Merrill smiled at her, said something. She hmmmed an answer, noncommittal, not sure what he'd said. She had been studying how the shadows crept up his sleeves. He didn't move. She didn't move. That earlier, subtle withdrawal circled in her thoughts, crying that it meant more than the discomfort of wet skin and clothing.

Her friends knew Merrill. A confirmed bachelor, they warned her, their voices light but their eyes steady as they watched for her reaction. He would never make room in his life for the complications of another's.

She realized that she was humming, very lightly, something that made Merrill focus on her face.

"Sorry," she said.

"I was just trying to figure out what that was."

She couldn't remember.

"Are you bored?"

She said no. Really, she wasn't, and what would they do if she said she was? She had a horror that he would hunker down at one of the low cupboards to find a faded Monopoly board from his childhood, or Parcheesi.

Jane stared at the flame emerging from the downturned metal mouth of the lamp. A tongue from a mouth, the flame rising from the wick as wide across and thin through as a ribbon. Or a sword. She remembered the apocalyptic vision, the King of Kings, and from his mouth issued a sharp sword with which to smite the nations.

An old apostle rustled. Put on the whole armor of God. Woman, keep silent, and guard against wantonness. Jane twisted in the ghost-grip of her mother's religion. Her own failed marriage, the silence that greeted her decision to leave. Now this relationship – how she despised that bloodless word – this love affair. Merrill was free of old pains like hers. No failures. A sweet sleeper, untroubled.

She realized what she had been humming.

"From strength to strength go on,
  Wrestle and fight and pray;
  tread all the powers of darkness down,
  And win the well-fought day."

Wesley. She loved the martial hymns, with armor and swords, not the ones about penitence and waiting and hoping. No pie in the sky for the meek. The strong would have to bleed for heaven, battling their way back up the sky from the fallen earth.

∾

It was getting dark again, with thunder.

"It's coming back around," Merrill said.

"Is the phone out, too?"

He reached over to the marble-topped table where a black telephone squatted, decades out of date. He lifted the receiver and held it out. Dead.

"Usually when one goes in a storm, they both go. Sometimes the phone is really gone. A couple of days."

"What about your practice?"

"They'll shift my calls to someone else. They know I live out."

He didn't seem concerned. Jane wondered how he could be so passive when the air was so charged. Floods and downed lines, wind and storm. He was phlegmatic as a farmer watching hail chew through his crops.

The rain started again, a few drops, then a steady rain, and through it the lightning and thunder marching just north of the house.

Jane got up and stood at the window. Flashes illuminated a chair in the back yard, a swing. The abandoned tool shed. Merrill's farm truck. In the black between the lightning-flashes, her face appeared on the glass, pale and round as one of the peonies in the untended borders.

The gutters burbled as the rain came heavily, and water leaped into the matted grass from the end of the downspout.

Her car waited in the garage. Jane pictured herself driving through the spreading pool despite the warnings, the danger. The unseen bridge solid under her tires, the water parting from the forward force of the car. A creamy wake closing behind her as she made her way through.

Cool air blew past her, pushing away the cloying scent of lamp oil. She smelled flowers fading at the overgrown edge of the woods.

Jane ran her fingers over the frame of the window, the roughness of paint over paint over paint.

∾

Something was banging at the door, clattering the screen door into the frame. Jane stepped back from the window, looked to Merrill.

"Skinner's at the door."

He pushed out of the couch and went to the hall that opened onto the front porch. She heard the door open, heard him talk but the words were indecipherable, a coaxing sound. He came back followed by the rolling bulk of the dog.

Skinner stopped between the rocking chair and the couch. His eyes, black in the black fur, gleamed as he turned his heavy head toward her, then toward Merrill who was already back on the couch. He seemed to want something, waiting, expectant. Finally he went down on his elbows and crawled under the heavy coffee table, where he sighed once and then went still.

A siren worked up the scale.

"Gardiner. The fire department."

In a little while, a second fire siren began to wail, closer by. It was joined by klaxons and other sirens. "That's the Acklin station," he said, slowly, like a sage finding the syllables by touch in the warm guts of a bird. "Somebody's got a fire, or a bad wreck."

Darkness filled the valley like water finding a new level. The sleeping forest merged with the sky, sticks and thickets that faded black into blue-black.

She looked at his hand resting flat on the upholstery, how his thumb forked sharply away from the span of his fingers, like a road that must be followed.

The glaring lamp.

The motionless world.

His eyes.

Her newly wetted lip.

HOUSECLEANING

 ～

NAN VOGELSANG SPENT HER EVENINGS AND WEEKENDS cleaning up what he left behind.

He left on a Tuesday and never looked back, let the attorneys handle it. Of course, they never visited the dim half-finished basement to cart out the board-ends and old lumber, glue gone bad in the tube, carpet squares, wire nuts, a rake without a handle, loose Allen wrenches, a hacksaw with the blade worn smooth and useless. None of this was mentioned in the legal documents.

Or the bent nails, thrown back in the blue cardboard boxes along with the good ones. Pounds of nails, spikes and finishing nails, roofing nails and decking nails. More than anything else, nails.

And the sandpaper discs, clotted with blackened shellac. An old picture frame, come apart at opposite corners into two right angles. A pair of shears, rusted. Washers. Stove bolts. A can opener with grease on the handle. The start of a butcher-block table top, the edges raw and top unfinished. Sockets loose from their set. A gallon of neatsfoot oil. PVC joints. Brick-colored rags tossed under the work bench. A square of plexiglass. A nearly empty can of WD-40. The kitchen wall clock that buzzed and stuck. A broken kite. A wall calendar from the gas station. A Phillips-head screwdriver with a broken tip, used for mixing and prying, the end gobbed with tar. Flux and a roll of solder and the torch but no propane. Paint sticks. Miniature dunes of sawdust swept aside by his hand.

Now he was gone gone gone. Gone to another life, like a cicada coming up out of the ground after nine years. That was how he'd explained things to a friend, who by way of other friends brought the story back around to her.

He had flown away, she thought, or crawled, but the discarded shell remained. And it was supposed to be seventeen years.

She couldn't see how the marriage had been cut off so abruptly; neither could she project ahead the time they might have spent together. The years fell away to both sides. All she could see, if things had not changed, for more years, or ever, was that eventually they would have been swamped with the accumulation of George's things. And maybe that's why he left, she thought as she filled another box. Rusted trowel. Wood putty. One glove with the thumb broken through. He wasn't able to deal with the complexity of the accumulated and undiscarded.

His parents were country people who got factory jobs but continued to live surrounded by acreage they rented to people who still milked cattle and grew corn. In their world, you didn't throw things away that might be used for propping or filling, holding or patching. It was a useful trait among people like those whose farms had been sliced into lots for this new subdivision. In the suburbs, thrift was a liability. A box of things you might need was like an appendix, or tonsils, without purpose, only problematic.

A round red reflector disc, the glue on the back gone brittle. A chunk of two-by-four. Electrical tape. Handles from an old filing cabinet.

Nan had never intruded on his shop. She knew how he worked, everything strung out across the workbench, and anything picked up or moved could set a project back for hours, or forever. The sheer number of things here had put her off for months, while she soldiered through the financial shifts and legal matters. She'd donated sporting goods to the Scouts and carted his abandoned clothes to Goodwill, lowering the bags into the drop-off bin and then racing home – hoping people in the shopping center believed her to be a young widow.

She pulled out a coffee can with a trim brush dried to the bottom, tossed it in the box. This disorder was so much a part of him that, with George gone, the vitality was gone, too. There'd been hopefulness in his hoarding.

Nan hefted the box and climbed the basement stairs, threw her hip against the door to hold it open while she shifted the box across to the cargo deck of the van backed close against the house. She pushed the box against the others already there. Grass brushed high against her ankles, one more thing that needed doing.

She brushed flakes of rust from her hands, went back down and started on the paint cans. She shook each one in turn, some of the gallons so light that they swung high in the air when she pulled them from under the workbench. There were pint cans of stain they had moved from their last house, now thick as syrup. Finally, she went down on one knee to peer under the bench, finding dust, a spool of string for the weedwhacker, and a dead cricket.

What was that? She reached with a yardstick and scraped at something black on the wall. Nothing moved. It wasn't an insect or spider. Nan poked her head into the recess.

The back of the workbench had a scrap of flakeboard nailed against the uprights to keep cans from sliding off the shelves. The rough surface was scrawled with black china marker, columns of large figures in George's familiar handwriting. Sevens that looked like ones, all the numbers slewing with the lope of a bear on a down slope, gaining speed.

Nan took hold of the board and yanked. It creaked against the nails that held it. She squatted and put both hands to the board, pulled steadily. The flakeboard groaned and then gave all at once, and she went half onto her back, rocked forward with the piece of board in her hands. The edges were splintered where compressed fragments of wood broke apart under pressure. She rolled to her knees, her head thrust forward under the workbench, and saw the place the board had been. The bare block wall was visible now, dull gray like something dead, like a bad tooth. Like the socket where a bad tooth has been removed.

She tossed the board into the garbage box. The figures slanted across. Calculations for two-by-fours, how many needed on 16-inch centers. Nan remembered the trucks from the lumberyard stacked with framing lumber and plywood.

Nan turned the board over, carried the box to the van. She slammed the back door closed. In the morning, she'd drive by the landfill and dispose of the mess.

But in bed that night, she kept seeing the scrawled numbers. Her skin itched, like after sunburn, like there'd been too much bleach in the wash. Like columns of ants adding toward some subterranean explosion.

~

The next morning, Nan went down to the workshop and began pulling tools from their wall hooks. Crowbar, pliers, a claw hammer with the cracked handle mended by duct tape. She swung the crowbar as she climbed the stairs, liking the heft of it, recalling through her skin how steel warmed to the hand, how wood handles felt oily from long use. Not since they built the place had Nan used tools in earnest – only for picture-hanging, or once, assembling a bed frame.

She knew there were other scribblings, curses cut into the memory of the house. Behind the wallpaper. On the joists under her feet and the rafters above. Nan stood in the living room. She didn't need to close her eyes to make the furniture disappear and the lamps and books, the barnboard paneling.

He's standing by the rough opening for the patio door, turned away from her after she'd failed at something he asked. The baggy seat of his jeans is dusty. He clenches a flat carpenter's pencil, maroon, the soft lead sharpened by a knife, and draws lines backward in that graceless left-hand style.

Nan put the flat prongs of the crowbar under a board. She leaned her weight against the curved opposite end. The gray board, though pocked with nail-holes and cracked by long-ago weather, was strong and popped its nails, one two three. She pried up the other end, then opened the sliding glass door and flung the board across the deck and onto the lawn.

The barnboard paneling was laid up in diagonal rows that met in the middle like sergeant's stripes. She pulled the boards free on one side from waist height to the ceiling, then started on the on the opposite row.

She was halfway up that side when the first marks appeared, a rough sketch of a door or window, and words. The names of suppliers? She couldn't tell, the letters illegible. On the dented white surface of the sheetrock, they looked like the scrawl of a ransom note, a threat wrapped around a brick and thrown through a window.

She pried up board after board, each a satisfying yield, and tossed them with a harvester's economy of motion out the door.

The neighbor's dog began to bark and gallop from corner to corner of his invisible fence. Nan heard the momentary race of a car engine being put into park. She stopped working and went to the front door.

Dave Oliver's red pickup was in the drive, and he was at the bottom of the stairs, looking up at her, one foot on the step, one on the ground. "Hey, Nan." He paused. "I was on my way to the home center."

He looked at her strangely, his crooked mouth always on the verge of smile but now pulled down as though he might sob. She felt a flash of anger – am I that pitiful – then realized that she held the crowbar across her chest like a weapon. Sweat cooled on her temples and she felt the shine of exertion on her face, the blood pumping under her skin.

Dave looked past her into the house. She turned, saw the gutted wall.

"I'm getting rid of a few things," she said.

"Remodeling?"

"Just – getting rid." She swung the storm door wide. "Come on in."

He walked over to the wall, his hands shoved down in the pockets of his cut-off khakis, and gazed at the sheetrock. He tilted his head, trying to read.

"Y'know, I thought I was pretty close to George, as neighbors go," he said. "We did things together. He helped me build that fence. But I met him in town not long after he moved out, and he put his head down and walked by. Didn't say a word."

Dave turned, and his eyes were dry but that didn't signify a thing. "Whatever was between you two was just that. He had no reason to act like he did."

He held out his hand. Nan gave him the crowbar.

He drove the flat end under the drywall and pulled. The board cracked all the way across and gypsum trickled from the edge.

Her husband's friend broke out the section with the writing, then the part above and below. An eight-foot section of the stud wall stood open, with the pink insulation and the wiring snaking through holes in the 2-by-6s.

Nan threw the pieces into the back yard as he attacked the next section of paneling. Nails screeched. After a little while, Dave began to hum.

~

She was too tired to shower, throwing herself into bed coated with gypsum dust and dried sweat. She could smell mildew and the raw vinegar drench of wood wrenched apart.

Her body ached, her shoulders and thighs. She rolled from side to side. Her hair fell into her mouth, tasting foul, and she pulled it from her dry lips with dusty fingers.

Outside, crickets repeated things she would listen to, if she didn't respect herself more. They sawed and sawed, and late in the night a screech owl whinnied from a tree close by. George had left in late winter. It was summer. August.

Nan cried, the tears sliding silently down her face. The racking sobs that had left her breathless and strengthless had stopped, sometime in the spring.

She saw the living room wall, bare, and despaired of what she'd done. What was left to do.

After having avoided looking into them so long, she wasn't sure if she could take the comfort of people's eyes.

~

The next morning, Nan ate breakfast on the back patio, overlooking the pile of debris. Heavy dew had spotted the drywall. It beaded on a spider web strung between three angled boards.

She wasn't surprised to hear Dave's truck again. Whatever barrier there had been, whatever taboo or taint of uncleanness had clung to her abandonment, was broken. She was surprised, however, to see two other men crammed into the front seat of the Toyota.

"I brought help," Dave called.

"I see."

Rick had been another of her husband's neighborhood friends, from one street over; Angelo made up the occasional foursome for golf or a bowling night. They nodded at her, stood with their hands on their hips, surveying the house, squinting against the sun that rested just above the ridgeline like a second horizon crossed that morning.

The men carried their own tools. Dave wore a leather belt with hangers, hammer, screwdrivers, pliers, nail-puller. Angelo had a Craftsman tool box with drawers, and all the tools inside had red handles and were set into their proper places. Rick's tools slid and crashed inside a primer-gray metal box, its lid sprung from some accident.

They started by carrying all the living room furniture down into the yard. The leather couch, pole lamps, baskets. The recliner opened after they set it down, as though a family invisibly took its ease on the front lawn.

Dave set a boom box on the kitchen counter and Springsteen came full-throated from the speaker.

Down came the paneling, the rest of the weathered boards on the second side of the room. Then the drywall, bare or painted. The tools scraped and the men sang along with the parts of the songs they knew.

While they dismantled the living room, she started emptying the kitchen cupboards, climbing on the stepladder to reach far back on the upper shelves. Nan tossed down plastic butter tubs, picnic dishes, cracked cups. She found a Christmas plate deep in the back, forgotten, and set it in the sink.

The small cupboards over the refrigerator were hard to reach. That's where she found the red glass wine carafe received as a wedding gift, etched with roses and their initials, too gaudy for words. She scraped her arm against a cabinet edge, reaching for a set of spice jars still in their flimsy carton.

She sucked at the broken skin and welling blood. Her own salt taste was familiar. The cutaneous heat of the scrape brought back all the bruises, cuts and splinters suffered in building this house with their own hands. Insulation had prickled in her skin for days after she stapled the pink batts into place. Grime caked inside her elbows. Spattered paint went unnoticed until Monday afternoon at her desk, when she bent to pick up a paper and saw the spray of fine white spots across her instep.

She had focused on the good ache of work, in her muscles and tendons, because the other ache couldn't be spoken of.

Nan could never tell if something was straight, the chalk lines climbing and diving away from her as she looked. It was a constant incapacity. If she anchored a tape measure, it twisted. If she hoisted a board, its weight would slowly sink in her untrustworthy hands until his hammer drove the nail home with the edge just off level.

His harsh words drove her failure deep inside, until she didn't trust her body to move properly, until her eyes couldn't be believed. Until she had to do things over and over, patting inanimate objects into place lest they move when she turned away.

The men ordered pizza for lunch. She paid the girl who delivered it, and they sat down cross-legged on the carpet to eat right out of the box. Angelo did his Italian schtick when he went for more drinks, singing "O Sole Mio" and miming an accordion. He had a thick neck but small, precise feet. Dave spun the little three-legged stool that kept the lid off the pizza toppings, making it clatter across the cardboard.

They moved to the kitchen. She moved to the guest bedroom. A 20-year-old song came on the radio and she danced as she took down the curtains, lifting each hook from its slot in the traverse rod.

The men rolled away when the heat of the day was beginning to fade, the leaves on the maples spreading as the sun went down.

The living room was bare, a cell, clean as an archeological excavation. Windows, studs, siding. The insulation had disappeared, and the wiring. The dining room was the same. In the kitchen, they had taken down the cupboards and removed the sheetrock, then pushed the appliances back into their places.

As the sun faded and the living room turned moon-colored with the glow of the streetlight through the bare windows, she went into the bath and ran a deep tub of steaming water. She poured herbal beads into the water. The back wall of the bathroom was the appliance wall of the kitchen; she could see the stamped steel and printed diagrams and coiled gas supply lines like organs through the framing.

Nan immersed her arms in the oil-filmed water, easing the scrapes and cuts. She squeezed out a sponge over the sore extent of a muscle. Her narrow knees flexed and extended like something remote and powerful.

Her skin shone. Shone like sweat. George had talked about sweat equity, his investment, recovering his investment.

She had made an investment, too. Now she was getting it back, a piece at a time.

She lay down in the bed, her skin smooth against the white sheets.

She lay with arms outspread and legs apart, in the middle of the king-sized bed. Her skin breathed oil and herbs into the linens, the image of her body radiating into the fabric, the heat of her body sealing a resinous imprint that would remain when she rose.

~

Nan used a pair of pliers to pull up the carpet.

The installers had stretched it across the floors and fastened it to tack strips along the walls. The points of the tacks would prick her bare toes when she crossed a threshold or pressed her feet right up against the wall.

The carpet made a satisfying rip as she yanked it from its moorings. Dust that had seeped down over the years made little gray drifts along the wooden strips. In some places the padding stuck to the plywood. She remembered picking out this particular padding, not the very best but good, shreds of foam pressed into a continuous sheet eight feet across. Most of the foam pieces were pink or yellow.

Nan pushed the carpet back as she worked, until a section was free. She rolled it loosely and dragged it to the back door, heaved it off the deck onto the lawn. In that short drop it unfolded into a neat ensign, half brown jute, half sculptured champagne polyester.

The padding followed, floating out and settling its Easter colors over the carpet and the uncut grass, very green in the long light of early morning.

The floor now was nothing but splintery plywood stamped with obscure names and blurry symbols, trees and triangles, in the colors of ink that are pressed into government-inspected hams. And pencil-marks, numbers, doodles, good intentions.

Dave had left his radio. She turned it up loud, stomping on the underlayment, the hollow basement booming, the bare rooms echoing. She danced with her feet apart and her arms waving above her head. Her body was levers and pulleys, muscles working against bone, and she felt a warm sweetness as she whirled and kicked.

That night, she slept on the bare floor in the bedroom, the comforter rolled around her like a sleeping bag. The house was open to the warm breezes, again, little brown bats navigating through the skeleton, the stars moving across the spaces where windows had been.

~

The Saturday work party arrived with galvanized tubs, ice, cases of beer and soda. Angelo and Dave and Rick had brought their friends, neighbors, wives and kids. Someone's mutt lolloped back and forth, barking.

All that stood any more at 16 Morris Lane was the house's skeleton under a roof stripped of its shingles and plywood. The low hills beyond, the other houses on their acre lots, were framed by the 2-by-4s and the isosceles triangles of the trusses.

A limber boy, his chest still smooth, shinnied up one corner to attach a chain to the trusses.

Nan started up the other side. She clenched the wood with her sneakers and knees, slowly working her way to the angle of wall and roof, clinging there while she pulled up the heavy chain with the cord she'd tied to her waist.

She looked past the corner, through to the trees into the garden where Tim and Karla bent, unconcerned, over their plantings, and far away to the river glinting as it bent west. She looped the chain around the truss and fastened it with the clamp. The boy half slid, half leaped from his corner, but she paused, aware of the 10 feet to the ground, that a mistake would mean a broken ankle, a splintered collarbone. She crabbed to the railing, then leaped from there to the ground.

Two trucks rolled carefully away from the house, until the chains went equally taut at their trailer hitches. Then, with a starter's signal from Dave, they gunned forward, tires spinning, and the trusses creaked, cracked, fell, bringing the shell down with them, the whole thing slumping into the cellar hole.

The squares and angles were broken. The violence of nails and screws was ended. Words that had welded the whole thing together went back into the air, into the syrup-colored light. As the dog barked and the crowd cheered, dust rose in thinning clouds, like newly hatched gnats flying upward on the warm air.

TROUT

~

CALLIE UNWRAPPED her tropical print skirt and draped it across the chair. She unbuckled her sandals and kicked them gently toward the bed.

Sightseeing was work. She promised herself that she would slip away from the tour tomorrow morning, find some pretext to stay at the hotel and lounge by the pool. Perhaps a touch of indigestion.

She had seen enough of crumbling Spanish forts and colorful markets where the people pressed against you, smelling of onion and fish, demanding that you buy baskets and hats and souvenirs.

The curtains were drawn against the afternoon sun, which struck blindingly up from the beach and the long blue ocean. The balcony doors were open a little, though, because the breeze came through and billowed in the curtains, making their green-and-gold pattern move like leaves in the wind. The sinuous pattern tangled like the shadows of leaves at noon, cast across the grass.

She sat on the edge of the bed and then lay back, her tired bare feet flat on the floor, her toes deep in the plush of the carpet.

Someone walked by on the sand below her window, carrying a radio. The song came up to her, passing through the curtains, a familiar song from a year ago. The words were distorted, barely seemed to be in English, seemed to be easing from English into the island patois. Could it be a remake of the song? But no, she recognized the voice. Mary's 14-year-old daughter, next door, had played the radio all last summer while she lay on a lounge chair on the patio, gleaming with coconut-scented oil. That song and that rough-voiced singer were the same.

Callie reached up and unhooked the strap of her bathing suit at the nape of her neck. She rolled the suit down, the underpinning of the bra releasing her breasts. Then she arched her pelvis and let the suit slide to her ankles.

The bedspread, which also was green and gold, was smooth under her back. She felt cool and relaxed, lying there in a room where the half-darkness was soft and welcoming, moving gently with the inhale and exhale of the curtains. Organic, like the pulsation of living tissue.

The curtains lifted in a strong gust that whistled through the space between the glass doors.

The curtains of her home had puffed in and out at the open windows all summer long. White curtains, bleached and washed to softness, bloomed in every one of the tall, old-fashioned farmhouse windows. At night, when the house breathed out the day's accumulated heat, the curtains flared like petals, flowers opening on an evening primrose.

She still thought of it as home, that childhood home, the spare old gray house standing between two wide fields, with its two aging trees and bank of day lilies beside the road. The house itself was gone, now, torn down to extend the fields seamlessly one into the other. And she was gone from it, separated by more than thirty years and a few other things that had been torn down as well.

She could feel the minute changes in temperature as the air swirled through the room. Her skin had been abraded by sun and wind and water until it was thinned right to the nerve-ends, and she could sense things that before would have been too fine to pass through for the callus of her daily skin.

Her body cooled, releasing the heat of the day. Her nipples tensed.

It was pleasant being naked, free of the belts and straps that confined her normal self. It was something like, but far better than, the sensation of swimming, with the water coursing past her arms and slipping past her throat and through the clinging fabric of her suit. In the ocean, the surf drove against that thin wall of modesty, pressing and sucking, urgent.

Callie could not remember when she had last been purely naked. There had always been so many others – parents, brothers, Harry who was now gone (oh, the banality of it, his announcement that he was in love with his secretary) and Little Harry who was grown and gone also. Neighbors who threatened to drop in unannounced at any hour between morning coffee and nightcap.

This daytime nakedness in the wide privacy of her own room was delicious.

"Come on, Lydia!" A young man's voice, below on the sand.

"Caledonia!" The soft, age-washed memories of her home were suddenly stark, as though a brilliant bolt had driven past unthreatening clouds to make everything bright as a camera's sudden flash.

"Caledonia!"

The gray old house, standing alone in the summer buzz of the hayfields, apart from the world as if separated by a desert or an ocean. She lay on her back on a torn quilt, in the back yard where the sun had burned the wiry grass brown and where brown grasshoppers sprang from patches of bare dust. A radio played in the house and her mother sang with it, slightly behind the music, her unsure voice wavering on the long sad notes.

Callie wore shorts, and a sleeveless blouse that she had unbuttoned and folded back. She didn't want to go back to school with a farmer's tan like all the other country girls, their brown skin giving way to white at shirtsleeve length and pointing in a vee from throat to breastbone. In the showers, the farm girls stood like strangely marked African animals while the sleek town girls compared their perfect bathing-suit tans.

She woke to see Tom Harkness, the tongue-tied son of the farmer two miles down the road, standing over her. Even if he could have said anything, which was doubtful, he didn't. He stood there with his lean shadow falling across her legs.

"Caledonia!" Her mother's voice shocked them both. Callie sat up suddenly, her cotton blouse creased wetly to her back, and Tom turned and ran.

Her mother's voice was not angry, but frightened, and Callie realized that there was something frightening and powerful in her self, something that made her mother cry out and a shy boy run, crashing like a deer through the tall hay.

Callie was shaken by the immediacy of the memory. A heaviness settled in all her body, like when the stingray had glided past her in the surf, lashing its barbed tail, and she had been sure that she was stung and poisoned because of the sudden weightiness of her movements. It was a poison that made her aware of the presence of every single layered cell, every molecule of her body, a live poison.

She lay perfectly still on the bed. She was as old now as her mother had been that afternoon. She was frightened now as her mother had been, knowing that the power of bare flesh in the sun is temporary, passing away like water, that it is leached away in childbearing and wifehood.

And yet. And yet.

In her skin now, despite that long-fought slackness of middle age, Callie was more alive than she had been in years. It was not sexual, this sensitivity to the feel of the air on her body. It was no more sexual than fish swimming, but there was that same aliveness as a fish in water.

Fish tasted with their skins. There was a line along their smooth sides where they tasted the water and all that was in it.

She had seen trout, in a clear Adirondack stream, aligned like arrows into the current. Their fins moved gently, steadying them in the water that enclosed them with the sensation of touch and taste and smell all together.

"I wish you'd walk more carefully," Harry had complained. "Trout can feel vibrations from the ground."

The breeze off the water lifted the curtains. The bright pattern moved like waves. Not like trees, or leaves of trees, but like water.

Callie closed her eyes.

She saw herself parting those curtains and stepping out onto the balcony, facing the afternoon sun.

Like a swimmer she parted the currents of air, tasting with her vibrant skin the clear, delicious flow that surrounded her and that she breathed in and made a part of her flesh forever.

CONTROL

~

Erica turned the key in the lock, opened the door, paused before she entered.

Nothing. Light poured in, the floor gleamed amber. Nothing but ceaseless bright silence unmarked even by the hum of the refrigerator.

The storm door swung shut behind her, almost catching her. She set her purse, keys, and mail on the table. No way to tell if the plumbers had been there, like the crew that came to her last rental and left notes from a Doodle Pad with empty faces to be filled in all around the border.

She walked to the bathroom. The towels hung straight. The tile was clean.

Erica lifted the tank lid from the commode. A new mechanism had been installed. Instead of the rusty old flapper that leaked water in the night, this was a whole unit in plastic, white and a bright medical blue.

She put the lid back with a dry scrape of unglazed porcelain edges, jiggled it until it set properly.

As she glanced down, the last check that everything was secure, she saw the mark. A black thumbprint on the side of the tank, in grease or trap-sediment.

Erica looked on the other side to find two smeared fingerprints.

She squatted in front of the commode. Touched the marks that clearly showed the oval of his thumbs as though the plumber had knelt and spread his hands against each side, holding it steady.

~

Erica did her chores.

She took a bag of spinach from the crisper and spent half an hour sorting the firm dry leaves from the fecal mess at the bottom of the bag. She parted leaves from stems, washed the leaves and shook the water from them. Patted them dry, then made a salad with mushrooms and slices of herbed chicken.

She preferred eating alone at her own table to eating alone in a restaurant. After dinner she patterned out her bills and paid them as a documentary droned on the TV behind her, so without action that the light didn't even flicker past her onto the wall.

Later, getting ready for bed, she washed her face and brushed her teeth. Remembered that she had a dental visit next week and looked for floss.

When she opened the door to the medicine cabinet, a roll of yellowing bandage spilled out.

Erica set it back on the shelf. The cabinet looked unbalanced, the bottles and tubes all to the left.

She pushed vials of outdated antibiotics along the shelf. The plastic clicked, as it must have when the plumber thumbed the amber bottles back and forth, must have used his thick fingers to turn them, read the labels.

Erica opened the door to the linen closet, released the flowery scent from the dryer sheets. Opened the door under the vanity, the cleaning products all white-bottle innocent beside the trap. Pulled open the drawers where she kept her secret things, female things. The musty smell was the smell of a man.

∼

"What you need is a wife."

Erica shook the water from her fingers and pulled a length of towel from the dispenser. "I had a husband."

"No, a wife is different." Shelly leaned close to the mirror, picked at an imperfection on her round chin. "A wife stays home and sits around waiting for deliveries and repairmen."

"Like a watchdog. Nice."

The tall woman from accounting came in and went into a stall without a word. Shelly made a mouth at the closed door.

Erica and Shelly stood side by side, putting on lipstick. Erica's, plum.

Shelly's, clear pink like the waxy junior lipsticks they got when they were girls.

"Well, it was a strange feeling," Erica said, watching the shape of her mouth as she spoke. "I mean, who was this man? He was in my house. I wouldn't know him. He could be walking back and forth on my street for all I know, every day."

The rest room echoed with the flush and then wide-open spigots as the accounting woman washed her hands thoroughly, and dried them. She glanced at Erica, smiled and left.

"What did he do?"

"He fixed the faucet on the vanity."

Shelly made a fat little fist around her thumb and swung at Erica's shoulder in the illusion of a roundhouse punch.

"What did he DO?"

Erica shrugged. "I don't know. What do they do in empty houses? It just felt like he'd been there. The stuff in the medicine cabinet was moved around."

"Everybody does that anyway."

Erica looked cornerwise at her. Shelly was adjusting her bra, lifted the cups under each breast.

"Maybe it's nothing. I could feel that someone had been in the house, that's all. It's not like he went through my underwear."

Shelly gave a pained look. "Damned thing." She pulled at a strap, lifted her chest. She's wearing a Wonderbra, Erica thought. She deserves what she gets.

"Like I was saying," Shelly said, "I don't let anyone in my place, rental agency or not, unless I'm there."

"Easier said than done."

"Do what I did," said Shelly. "You'll feel better. I found out."

Erica waited for the tone of outrage to resolve into incident. "So what happened?" she finally asked.

"I came back to the condo when an air conditioning crew was working. They were in my kitchen eating cookies. My Girl Scout cookies. With their elbows on the table."

~

Erica made coffee.

She opened the folding louvered doors to the pantry and browsed along the shelves for cereal, bagels, anything. She rattled a few spoon-size biscuits in a box.

The machine finished burping and choking on the coffee. She waited, impatient, the drops sliding free of the hole under the filter until she pulled the pot out and the last two or three fell to sizzle on the warmer.

She filled her mug. As she lifted it, the sun caught the blue veins under her wrist, the hollows that momentarily held the dark. She remembered how the dark used to linger in her skin. That was years back, the nights she and Mike made passionate love. Pain filtered through her overexcited skin, sharp intake of breath. Raising the bar, the vault higher and higher, the next day the blue bruises on wrists, ribs, thighs. The tenderness of her study as the bruises faded green, to yellow, crushed blood metabolizing to waste.

She shook open the newspaper.

The president declaimed. Soldiers aimed their guns at an immobilized tank. A 20-car wreck in the fog in California.

Far back in the A section she read a long story about a man testing some kind of high-altitude balloon flight. His craft was as tall as an office building but looked like an organ, a gland cut free from the earth. He had to use oxygen and heaters, rising so high the horizon purpled to space.

Her husband's first departure was the withdrawal of the impression his body made on hers. Their fandango of planted knees and bared teeth stepped back to a minuet, fingertips touching, cool air eddying in the gap that grew wider, more formal. As she rinsed out her coffee cup, Erica watched the water swirl down the drain.

She thought about the plumber, in her house, opening the doors. Leaving marks on the porcelain like carbon streaks after fire.

~

On Thursday she saw the most stunning man riding in a plumber's truck.

At first she thought it was a girl. The face was long and modeled close to the fine bones, the eyes large, slanted and pale. Long hair curled and flowed out the open window.

But when she pulled next to the truck at a light, she saw the small stubble on his cleft chin, the slight growth of a beard. She could not imagine this man, this angelic man, with blackened hands and burns and sewage on his blue shirt.

She'd been watching vans and trucks. Reading the names lettered down their sides, plumbers, carpenters, carpet layers. And the men, their faces animated as they sang along with the radio as they drove, or slack as they rode slumped on the passenger side.

Most of the faces were unremarkable. One had been brutal. And now, this beautiful one.

The truck moved beside her car, light to light, moving a length ahead. The image of the man's face shimmered, otherworldly, as the side mirror vibrated with the uneven throb of the motor. She paced the truck for several blocks until she realized that they had turned west, away from her route. Erica swung across the lanes, left at the next light onto an unfamiliar street, wrong way on a one-way. She ratcheted her car down alleys and side streets until she was back on her usual route.

Perhaps he had rifled through her vanity and cabinet. He had lain on her bed motionless, so ethereal that his body did not leave an indentation.

A whirl of leaves came off the beaten ground of a tiny park with benches, into the street, swept clean across.

At work, the lunch-hour vision forgotten in the press of things to do, Erica worked without distraction. But at 4 p.m. she lifted her face to her own image in the rest-room mirror, and the wide stare appalled her.

She called the rental agency, reminded them who she was, the house on Glenview. The rental agent cooed, of course, of course, her voice pitched low and sweetly Southern.

"I wanted to know, who did the work on my bathroom?"

"Is there a problem?" The agent drew on all her reserves of empathy. "We'll have them right back out there, now, if there's some problem."

"No, not that. I have a friend who needs a plumber, someone she can trust in her house." Erica could see Shelly's face, her quick wounded cynicism. "She lives alone."

"Well, it's Frohman Brothers, they're even on your side of town if she's nearby. That's who we usually call, oh nine times of out 10. Very reliable. That was who we called for your little problem and I'm so glad it's fixed."

The name was not the one on the truck with the beautiful youth.

The way home took her by Frohman Bros. Plumbing. She saw the trucks, the name in black blocky capitals, before spotting the modest white sign over the office. Two men were working beside a truck in front of an open bay. Were they the Frohman brothers? They were middle-aged, seats bagging in their overalls, bald spots nearly the same on their round heads.

They were loading a hot water tank. The older one, from the grizzle of his hair, steadied the appliance as it rode down on an elevator at the back of the truck. He glanced up as she drove by, and then went back to the work at hand.

$\sim$

In the end, she ended up calling Frohman Bros.

She loosened the ring on the trap under the sink until water wept silently along the curve and onto the floor.

Erica would know, now.

She would see what they did. Their tinkering in the wet guts of things, pulling things free, tearing apart the mazes where it all ended up.

Erica hid in the pantry. She pulled one of the stools from the breakfast bar into the space, sat far enough from the louvered doors not to be seen, but so that she could see through the hinge space.

The truck came on time, roaring just before it was shut off. The plumber let himself in with the key from the agency, walking heavily.

Erica thought of the older brother, his frizzled hair around the tanned bald spot, committing transgressions in her home. Talking on her telephone. Drinking from the orange juice jug in the refrigerator, his hands pressing in the sides until the container splashed juice down his throat.

Nothing was unimaginable.

The man came into view, carrying a toolbox, set it down on the mat in front of the sink. It was another man, younger but not young. Lean in the way some men became not long after high school, corded and tough and ageless once they had leathered into themselves.

He was silent as she, not a whistler or a hummer of old tunes.

He opened the doors under the sink and looked in. Not for too long. He turned on the water and watched, saw the sliding drops spin free of the plumbing and down to the bottom of the cabinet.

Erica could feel herself rocking slightly on the stool, rocking with her heartbeat and her carefully controlled breath. She was the secret behind the closed door.

The plumber sat cross legged on the floor. His shirt hung loose over the hollow of his back and then went taut as he leaned forward. He turned the fitting, his hands moving like a woman's when she peeled around an apple. He took a rag and wiped everything dry, then touched his finger to the pipe the way a woman might test a cake.

He stood up, turned on the water. Turned it off, and checked the fitting again. Fixed.

He closed up his toolbox, unneeded, and then used his rag to carefully wipe the kitchen tiles where he had sat. The plumber mopped back and forth, folded the rag in a neat square and went back over the area.

Erica sat holding her breath in the slitted darkness of the pantry until the sound of the truck was gone.

Then she went to the sink and turned the water on, watched it go down the drain. Turned it off. Back on. Off.

CRUNCH

~

How could she be sure?

Anna opened her hands on the steering wheel, palms flat against the gray leather. She breathed out.

A flash of white. A child's head, hair still the color of milk but destined to fade, going under the bumper.

How could she know that it happened, that it didn't happen?

~

She was six hours into the trip, driving out of a dark damp late summer morning, fog lying over the fields. Syrupy dawn. Coffee and a biscuit in paper for breakfast, more coffee in the squinting 10 a.m. light as the heat shimmered into place. It was just before noon when she pulled off the road again.

The drive-through was awkwardly built, the turns too tight. She asked for a medium, something diet. We have Diet Coke. Okay, fine. The speaker crackled as the girl asked if that was large or medium, again. Medium. The car in front of her was at the service window forever.

Three bags handed over, opened, checked, the guy leaning out the window of his pickup. A wait, another bag.

Finally she was at the window. The girl fumbled her change. Anna took the drink and peeled wet paper from the straw, jabbed at the opening until it forced through. She looked in the rearview for someone coming around the building behind her and goosed forward, ahead of a pickup truck.

She accelerated, looking out toward the entrance and the noon hour traffic, around the corner of the building.

A whole family was straggled out across the parking lot. A teenager, head bent, a slash of hair across his eyes. Mom, Dad. Two kids of nearly the same age, holding hands. Grampa. Grandma. A girl, or a woman, maybe 16 but with her hips thrust forward as she walked and her breasts carried like eggs.

Anna leaned against the wheel, arms folded. Finally the last one was across. She gunned it, tires squealing momentarily as she cut the corner to the exit and out.

But as she crossed the highway, she looked back.

Had there been another child? Could there have been a small child running by himself, fine hair lifting up on even that little wind?

She had been looking at the girl, at her knowing strut, at her cheekbones and round forehead. Perhaps a child had been running after her. A child going under the car, his head just at the level of the molded black bumper.

Anna waited as the light cycled. Surely she would have felt the impact. Someone would have shouted, or run after her.

Still, she couldn't escape the reality of the vision. There had been no child, no jolt, no scream, no shocked faces – but she could see it all, the blond head and the bumper and the child thrown away from the impact, sleeping on the concrete after sudden violence, a trickle of blood from his ear.

~

Anna settled into the rhythm of the interstate. Already she had been six hours on the road, with 11 hours ahead. She planned to drive until dark, stop for the night, arrive the next day at the Linsbecks'.

The college was familiar only through Scott's letters. This was his fourth faculty position, each one taking him farther from their Pennsylvania undergrad days, mountain surrounds flattening into hills, into prairie. Forests into corn, now wheat. Eventually he'd roll up the foothills into the Rockies, she thought, a quick reprise of his journey, by then a full professor nicely graying into his place.

She might have followed the same path, if Tony hadn't lured her out of the Dickenson Library and into the hectic delights of commercial publishing. English department friends had joshed her for selling out, as they awaited word from chapbook competitions and jockeyed for new jobs at MLA, but the barbs had a point. She wrote blurbs and wooed authors, he did the deals, everything was fine.

After a while, she only kept up with Scott, a couple of others. When she became an agent, the word got around and she received some half-brazen, half-abashed inquiries from former classmates. Then Scott asked her to take part in the summer writers' conference.

"You can stay at our home. The guest housing is in desperate need of renovation," he'd written.

~

The sun slid down in front of her. Anna flipped the visor across the glare and the slicing light reflected from other cars' chrome like the blinding sweep of a flashlight into the darkness.

Fields stretched out and out, langorous with fertility and profit.

She looked deeply into the small towns as they went by, above or below the highway. Buildings with false fronts eying each other across empty main streets. Stop-and-go lights. Tractor dealers at each end of town, the arrays of red and green machines. A bus with the name of the school district blocked out in blue paint along the sides. The '60s-era church it turned toward, buff brick with a suggestion of a steeple in the upswept roof line, the imitation of stained glass in the blocks of color scattered across the windows.

She remembered the Koncheskys, the backs of their necks exposed in the pew in front of her. Their five-year-old had been killed when he darted into traffic.

There had been a party, visitors, kids playing and yelling. A moment of inattention and the child ran toward someone on the opposite sidewalk. The driver was not at fault. Maybe he was going 30 instead of 25. The kid came from between the parked cars, out of nowhere, and the street was steep. Maybe the driver's glance had slipped away, following a bird, or he had leaned over to change the station on the radio. It made no difference. The child was dragged under the wheels.

No one could put guilt onto the parents, not when Bob Konchesky sat with his white shirt scouring the shaved back of his neck. He and his wife, both bent, ready for the sword.

A flash of white. That's all there ever was. A moment when the sun shifted. The face appearing at a window, then nothing. A moment.

She saw the blond head, the bumper, the body. It was crazy. She was crazy. Nothing had happened.

~

Anna thought about the mockingbird.

It had flown low across the highway, and she'd braked, not too hard, the bird flashing across, its wing patches semaphoring. She was in a hurry. Maybe there was a sound. She looked in the rearview mirror but there was nothing on the highway, no sign of the bird.

When she pulled into the parking lot, and went around to put money in the meter, she found the mockingbird splayed across the grille.

One gray wing was thrust deep into the bars, the other spread like a hand. The bird was dead, its body real in a way that smashed things on the road are not.

Anna looked at it for a long time. Finally she leaned down and took three of the spread primaries between her fingers, pulled. The feathers slipped, soft vanes parting, the shafts firm but pliable as a stem. The body came away, but the other wing was still caught in the grill.

She'd pulled harder, a tiny crunch, and the mockingbird had fallen to the pavement.

~

It was not that he didn't want her to go. It was that he had accepted the long trip as if it were just the morning drive to work. Tony was not threatened by her visit to a college friend, not concerned. He helped her pack, tucking panty hose into the side compartment. He set the two alarm clocks – she always woke with the first, but worried that it might someday fail – but didn't get up as she showered and dressed.

Anna didn't want him to hold her back, but in a perverse way she would have appreciated it if he had tried.

She expected to miss him more. They had worked together for a long time, then she had begun her new career by working at home. She was there for him every evening. They had dinner together, without authors or editors. They became closer and closer.

Alone on the road, she saw the marriage getting smaller in retrospect, not larger. Tony receding, back and back. People driving by saw a woman alone. Single. Maybe always single. A white Jeep with suitcases, no sign of children. No car seat or toys, or bumper stickers about honor students.

~

The family at the drive-through had gotten out of a van. Could they all have fit in there?

She tried to think how many seats.

A big family. She hit the gas, caught the slow turning of Grampa's head at the noise.

Maybe his faded eyes widened as her bumper caught the running child, almost safe, his fingers reaching for the young woman's lowered hand.

The child was too small for her to see below the nose of the Jeep. Just the brief gleam of his hair. Then the sickening crunch of bones, the three-corner tilt as the front wheel went up and over. Like the thud and snap when she'd hit a squirrel or gone over someone else's unavoidable road kill.

Then the body on the pavement, the long eyelashes on the cheek, perfect in death.

~

She had seen Tony's face at the window. Just for a moment, the white round of his face, a bag pulled tight with a string. Then he turned away.

What made him wait until she was backing out of the driveway? She had said goodbye to him in the bedroom. As usual, he was rucked up in the sheets, only a corner of his face showing between comforter and pillow. Tony was awake, she said goodbye, he said to drive careful and call. She carried her own suitcases out to the garage.

It wasn't even the apparition of his face, illuminated by the streetlight as he stood close to the glass, but the way that he turned his face and body back to the darkness as her eyes met his.

The rituals of marriage had become merely habit. She clung to them because the alternative was black and threatening. Who was at fault? She couldn't see where she had let down in anything, any caring. In fact, she had become less and less demanding, her self fading, not doing things and truly not missing them, wanting him to be comfortable and secure and happy.

As an agent, she could pass as a housewife. She stayed home. The radio played. She went to the store in the afternoon to get fresh vegetables for dinner.

Surely she had done something, to make him look and turn away. Somehow she had slipped.

The sun burned directly in front of her, like a lighthouse her small craft was intent on meeting. Anna saw his face. She saw the child's head. The child had blue eyes, not brown like Tony's. The wide innocent acceptance of the bumper, the pain, the unconscious thwack against the pavement, already gone.

~

Her eyes burned. Anna pulled off at a rest stop, braking hard once she was out of the flow of traffic, the tires shimmying a bit on the frost-heaved asphalt. She pulled into a spot under a tree, shifted to park. She flexed her hands, aching from holding the steering wheel, and the knucklebones cracked and settled.

She had to pee, but first she walked around the front of the car, already expecting the heart-stopping moment when something lifted gently in the heat coming off the radiator.

Her hand came up, touched her lips; she thought how the unconscious movement was mimicked over and over again in fiction and film, but it was absolutely true.

She took a step, looked instead of glancing, and saw that the movement was from the wings of a butterfly.

Maybe it was still alive, just caught. Anna bent closer. It was a tiger swallowtail, yellow striped with black. The big wings fanned with the heat, and the ticking of the cooling engine was insect-like, a call or signal.

The wings rose and fell, ragged with impact and abraded by the wind.

∼

Another sign loomed overhead, passed. She went by exit after exit, the towns and road names meaningless, only the steadily decreasing exit numbers that told how many miles to the other end of the state.

Each exit was preceded by official blue signs with the logos of restaurants, gas stations and motels. She had planned to stop for the night, by mid-state at the latest. Anna counted the miles. Maybe six hours ahead of her, if she didn't pull off to eat. Her stomach was still full with the heat of the day, expanding.

She felt the road hum. She watched the gauges, the oil, the temperature. The radio station bickered with another, country with classical, and she pushed it off.

It would be early morning. She imagined Scott and Jae coming to the door, their faces moonlike with sleep. Frightened at the knock, they would peek out around the curtains, debating this stranger at the door. She wasn't expected. People stopped and called, people kept schedules, didn't turn into the drive with a sweep of headlights like a police cruiser arriving with bad news.

She should stop. Why not stop? But the light pulled her forward, the sun that had glared in her face all afternoon now sunk below the horizon, and the banded clouds fading from orange to rose to purple. She felt the dark rushing up behind her with the earth's rotation; she fled toward the last light.

A major highway intersected here. Restaurants glowed in parallel strips. Yellow and red and orange, sunset colors, also the colors that psychologists said made people want to eat and run. The windows of the restaurants were yellow, and inside their frames, people sat at tables and talked.

Anna felt a moment of wistfulness. It would be good to stop. To cradle a warm cup of coffee between her hands. The cup would be round and heavy, white stoneware, and when she turned it over the bottom would be marked with the outline of a buffalo.

Then she recognized how easily this came, this suspect emotion, a gesture. A false sense of home.

The white moment of a face at the window. Anna looked at Tony. She saw his face, but there was no recognition, no emotion. It was a face like that of a woman being left behind, passive, empty. A waiting face.

~

The child wore plaid shorts and some kind of pastel top, knotted at the waist. It might have been pink but the Kodachrome had faded. Her hair was white, cut short like a boy's because it was easier to take care of, under the circumstances. Her face was white with sickness.

She remembered having blonde curls. Her mother had told her that she liked red shoes.

But in this picture, the one that came floating up, she was standing alone in a summer yard, cut off at the knees.

Anna tried to place the year. The spruce tree over her right shoulder was dying, its branches turned to brown. She was going back into the hospital. It might have been 1962, or 1963.

She was holding the new stuffed bear that had been given to her by an aunt. Something to comfort her in the stark bare hospital room. The bear's plush body was clenched between her thin arm and her bony torso, the bear's eyes cheerfully askew.

She was looking straight into the camera. It was the kind of picture a parent takes, half in fear. If the child dies, at least there will be this last photograph. Mom or Dad pressing the button, angry with guilt and with the admission of that possibility, as though taking the picture could doom everything.

~

Something about her was reckless, now, driving on into the darkness. The world shrank to the white hood of the Jeep and the twin cones of light reaching ahead but never gaining any ground. Anything might be waiting, beyond the gape of those lights.

The highway was empty, a two-lane now, funneling her toward the small town and the red brick college and Scott and Jae, startled awake.

Anna watched the road, watching for eyes. The berm flashed with beer cans and broken glass, single bursts of light. Animals show pairs of reflections, two eyes, she thought, but remembered maimed cats and a hound born with one eye.

She didn't trust her vision. Everything glittered. Even the road surface scintillated. How could you know?

A few weeks ago, the paper had printed that story about the man on the hilltop. He was out late, walking along the highway. He was struck by a car at the very crest of the hill.

The first driver surely knew it was a man, but drove on. Maybe the next two or three realized, but panicked at the thought they might be blamed for his death. They kept going. After a while, his body became like a deer's, the intestines dragged pink along the asphalt, the hide rolled blackly into a ball, the limbs shattered.

He was a carcass, something red and bone-white, smeared across the pavement in the sudden glare of the lights as drivers hit the gas for that weightless moment as they topped the sharp hill.

Who could have seen the denim jacket, in the dark? It was a body, the lump of a body, streaked blood, and the white of bone without species or identity.